THE WEIGHT OF A HUMAN HEART

THE WEIGHT OF A HUMAN HEART

STORIES

RYAN O'NEILL

ST. MARTIN'S PRESS ❧ NEW YORK

THE WEIGHT OF A HUMAN HEART. Copyright © 2012 by Ryan O'Neill. All rights reserved. Printed in the United States of America. For information address St. Martin's Press, 175 Fifth Avenue, New York, N.Y. 10010.

Designed by Peter Long

www.stmartins.com

Library of Congress Cataloging-in-Publication Data

O'Neill, Ryan, 1975–
    The weight of a human heart : stories / Ryan O'Neill.—1st ed.
      p. cm.
    ISBN 978-1-250-02499-2 (hardcover)
    ISBN 978-1-250-02500-5 (e-book)
    I. Title.
    PR6115.N459W45 2013
    823'.92—dc23

                                                    2013010141

First published in Australia by Black Inc., an imprint of Schwartz Media Pty Ltd

St. Martin's Press books may be purchased for educational, business, or promotional use. For information on bulk purchases, please contact Macmillan Corporate and Premium Sales Department at 1-800-221-7945 extension 5442 or write specialmarkets@macmillan.com.

First U.S. Edition: July 2013

10 9 8 7 6 5 4 3 2 1

CONTENTS

THE WEIGHT OF A HUMAN HEART

COLLECTED STORIES

TWELVE STORIES (BEARSDEN PRESS, 1966)

My mother, Margaret Hately, was a short-story writer. In the few photographs I have of her she is carrying a book, holding it against her chest as if she were suckling it. There are no photographs of my father. My mother destroyed them when he left her, a month before I was born. I only know him from the parts of him she put in her stories – a limp, a way of reading the newspaper at arm's length. Whilst my mother wrote, my father was made of words.

When I was a child, I loved to watch my mother writing. She would sit at her scarred wooden desk under the stained-glass window in the hallway, the sunlight harlequinning the paper before her. Even now I see the top third of any page in a book as green, the middle blue, and the lower third as yellow. As she wrote, she would keep a cigarette burning in the ashtray at her elbow, occasionally blowing great smoky O's into the air. At these times I knew not to bother her. I liked to paint, and she never minded the mess as long as I was quiet. In my childish pictures my mother had eleven fingers, one of them being the pen she always held in her right hand. The morning was for writing and the afternoon for reading. She preferred dead authors to living ones; she wasn't as jealous of them. Still, she would weigh a book in the kitchen scales before reading it. 'Any book that weighs more than half a kilo isn't worth the trouble,' she said.

I learned very early that my name, Barbara, comes from the Greek word for foreigner. It's onomatopoeic, suggesting how the Greeks perceived the sound of other languages. Bar-bar-bar. My mother would often shake her head and say, 'Just because you're called Barbara doesn't mean you have to talk nonsense.' My father had chosen the name. Sometimes my mother would say to me, 'You look just like him,' but I never knew if this pleased her. I think she resented that my father had written half of me. He was killed in an industrial accident when I was six months old, and since he and my mother had never divorced, she received the compensation. With this money she was able to buy a five-acre block (her 'Writer's Block,' she called it) half an hour from Newcastle, and she built a house there, with lots of rooms and cupboards and hallways and bookshelves. There were so many places for hiding and eavesdropping, it might have been designed to stage Shakespeare's plays.

The Writer's Block was surrounded by a barbed-wire fence and had a large, untidy garden. Every day before dinner the two of us would do some weeding. I would happily pull up any green thing I saw, but my mother used some method I could never determine, taking a weed here, leaving one there. It was almost as if she were editing the garden. After dinner she would inspect my clothes to see if anything had been torn during the day, and I would stare at her eyes, which were a striking blue. The only make-up she wore was heavy black eyeliner. With her pencil, she would go over the lines again and again. Since she refused to learn how to sew, and hated to shop, she would buy all our clothes through the post. If I needed shoes, she would make me stand on top of an old, opened novel, then draw around my feet, cut around the tracing and send the footprints off to a shop in Sydney. The new shoes would arrive a few days later.

At bedtime my mother would lie beside me, and instead of 'The Three Bears' or 'Rumpelstiltskin', she would read aloud the story she had been working on that day, making corrections as she went along. Drifting into sleep, I listened to the stories in her first collection many times. When she wasn't at her desk, she was always making notes. I heard from one aunt that my mother had been writing about childbirth even as my head was crowning. She wrote ideas on cigarette packets, newspapers, even in the fog on the window. She would often forget where she had written something and then we would both search the house for hours, examining every scrap of paper we could find.

When I was five years old, I wrote my first and only book and gave it to my mother for her birthday. It was called 'The Horses of Rainbow Valley' and it was five pages long, bound with a piece of string I had found in the garden. It was full of drawings of fairies and spiders and flower petals. I presented the book to my mother, then watched as she took her red pen to correct the spelling and punctuation. Having written over almost everything, she returned the book to me. 'The structure is unsound, and the pacing is too slow,' she said. 'If you want to be a writer, you have to learn to rewrite.' I tore the book in half and started to cry.

There was one story in her collection that my mother never read to me at bedtime. It was called 'The Zebras of Cloud Valley' and it told of a young girl cheering her sick mother by writing a book for her. Critics consider it to be one of her most moving stories and it has often been anthologised.

A Serpent's Tooth and Other Stories (Penguin, 1980)

By the time I was thirteen years old, I had come to realise I would always be a minor character in my mother's life. She had never done more than sketch me in. When I found my birth certificate one day, while helping to recover more of her lost notes, I was thrilled. I had always hoped I was adopted and on the certificate, my mother's name was listed as 'Charlene Boag'. But when I showed her, she just laughed. 'That's me,' she said. 'Would you rather read a book by Charlene Boag or Margaret Hately?' She had become her pen name.

As a teenager, I was sick of books, sick of writing. I didn't like to bring my friends home because of the way my mother looked at them. She unconsciously measured people for a story as an undertaker might measure them for a coffin. One time, at dinner, after she jotted down something I had just said onto the tablecloth, I shouted, 'Can't you stop writing for one minute? I'm talking, not dictating!' I was old enough by then to understand her stories, and I hated the way she had killed my father in one of them, and how she had stolen the birthmark on my wrist and given it to a fictional girl, prettier and more bookish than me.

Once I was older, I began to notice my mother's cigarettes often contained something other than tobacco. When I asked her, she said, 'I'm researching a drug scene.' In the mornings when I found her asleep on the couch with two empty wine bottles, she would say, 'I'm researching alcohol.' I never introduced her to David, my first boyfriend. No men ever came to our house. My mother said the only men she wanted in her life were Hemingway and Salinger.

She eventually met David three days after my sixteenth birthday, when she came home unexpectedly from a conference. He and I were in bed together. 'What the hell is going on here?' my mother shouted and I screamed back, 'I'm research-ing fucking!' She left without another word. That scene became the climax for 'A Serpent's Tooth'. I read it in Sydney years later, after I left home.

I had no desire to study English as my mother wished. In fact, I was in danger of failing the subject at school. I just couldn't bear to open the books. I think my mother secretly hoped that by the time I went to university, her stories would be part of the curriculum and I would be required to read them along with Lawson and the rest. But I was a feminist. I didn't want to study the words of dead white males. ('I don't care about women's rights, only women's writing,' my mother said.) I wanted to be a doctor, and I was accepted to study medicine in Sydney. On the day I was to leave, my mother was sitting at her desk as usual, the light through the stained glass colouring the smoke that hung over her head.

'Ah, Barbara,' she said. 'What do you think of this? Is it too much?'

'I'm going now, Mum,' I said, shouldering my bag. 'David is giving me a lift to the station.'

She looked down at the paper in front of her.

'Wait, don't go yet. I love you,' she said.

'What?' I said.

She turned to look at me, breathing out cigarette smoke.

'This dialogue from the story. "Wait, don't go yet. I love you." Is it too much, do you think?'

'No, Mum. It's not too much,' I said. 'It's hardly enough,' and I left.

'Don't get pregnant,' she called from the window as we drove away.

I wasn't surprised when my mother killed me. The first time was a plane crash, the second I was burned alive, and the third was a swimming pool drowning. Even the critics took notice, with the *Sydney Morning Herald*, in its review of *A Serpent's Tooth* ('In just two collections, Hately has become our foremost short-story writer') wondering at the number of young women dying in her stories. It was uncomfortable visiting home around this time, thinking that even as she made small talk, or made lunch, my mother might be planning another murder. But there must have been a limit to how often a mother could kill her daughter, as after my fourth death (from choking on a chicken bone, in a story published in *Meanjin*), she let me live.

THE ABO AND OTHER STORIES (HATELY PRESS, 1986)

In my third year at uni, after I had read my mother's latest story (in which I lost my virginity yet again, and my father died once more), I decided to get a tattoo. I got drunk one night and went to a parlour in Kings Cross. Leafing through a book of designs in the cramped, dingy waiting room I eventually picked out a gothic 'Daddy's Girl'. The tattooist was only two or three years older than me, and he had a nervous way about him, as if he were afraid of being caught travelling through life without a ticket. I noticed he had paint under his fingernails. He looked at me and asked me if I was sure this was what I wanted.

'Yes,' I said. 'But I want you to misspell it.'

'What?' he asked. 'Why?'

'To make my mother angry.'

'She won't be angry enough if you get a tattoo?'

'No, only if it's misspelt.'

He laughed and I said, 'Stop looking at me. Do you want to paint my picture or something?'

'Maybe I do,' he said. He wouldn't give me the tattoo, but told me to think about it and to come back in a week's time and ask for him, Mark. If I was still sure, he said, then he would happily misspell and badly punctuate my arm. When I returned the next week, I didn't have the tattoo after all. But I went out with Mark. He was an artist. The only tattoo I have is of his name, which I had done the day before we were married. (My mother wouldn't come to the wedding. She was busy on a new collection, she said.) After the honeymoon I took Mark to visit my mother for the first time. It was two years since I had last seen her. She had grown wrinkled, like the spine of a book that has been opened too widely. Her hands were leprous with ink and nicotine, and the grey was showing in her hair. The garden had become overgrown, the colourful patches of native flowers choked by a strain of American rose that my mother had planted years ago. Mark at once offered to cut the bushes back, but my mother said, 'I like it like that. It reminds me of the modern short story. Would you like a beer, Mark?'

'No thank you,' Mark said. 'I don't drink.'

As soon as we were inside, I had to go to the bathroom. (I didn't know it then, but I was pregnant.) I sighed when I saw that there was no toilet paper, only a copy of the Arts section of the *Australian*. If my mother found an uncomplimentary mention of her work, this was her revenge. When I came out, and sat with Mark and my mother to afternoon tea, she at once noted the tattoo on my arm.

'So you sign your work,' she said to Mark. 'Are you sure I can't get you a beer? Wine? Something stronger?'

'Mark doesn't drink,' I said. 'He's told you that already, Mum.'

'I thought Aboriginals liked to drink. Aren't you an Aboriginal, Mark?'

'An Aborigine,' Mark said, glancing at me.

'And Barbara says you're an artist? I must say, Aboriginal art reminds me of those children's join-the-dots books.'

'Mum, don't,' I said. Mark took my hand.

'Well, Mrs Hately, they say a picture is worth a thousand words,' he said, looking at the rows of books on the wall. My mother lit another cigarette.

'I don't mind that Aboriginals didn't invent the wheel,' she said. 'But that they didn't invent the pen is a little backward, you must admit.'

'We also didn't invent Zyklon B, or nuclear weapons,' Mark said, watching my mother. She sat perfectly still, as if for her portrait.

'Well, the fact that we are talking in English right now, and not simply grunting at each other, shows which is the superior culture, don't you think?'

'My God,' Mark smiled. 'I knew you were a sour old bitch from reading your stories, but I had no idea ...'

'Are you sure I can't get you anything, Mark?' my mother interrupted. 'Pornography? Some petrol?'

'Mother, that's enough!' I cried, and I stood up, letting my cup of tea fall to the floor.

'It's all right, Barbara,' Mark said. 'At least she's saying it to my face. Usually her kind just whisper it as I walk by.'

'If you've read any of my stories, Mark, you must realise that I prefer direct speech to reported,' my mother said. She scattered some pages of the *Australian* onto the floor to soak up the spilled tea.

'I've read all your stories, Mrs Hately,' Mark said, taking down one of my mother's books, 'And you can correct me if I'm wrong, but I believe every one of your characters is as white as the paper they're printed on. For all your theories about Aborigines, I'm sure of one thing. You couldn't write a convincing Aborigine.'

'On the contrary. That would be as simple as an Aboriginal drawing of a man,' my mother said.

'Then that's one story of yours I might actually enjoy reading,' Mark said. 'Barbara is upset. We should be going. I don't believe that we'll meet again. But rest assured, I'll be happy to come for your funeral.'

'My dear boy,' my mother smiled, 'with the life expectancy of your people, I will probably come to yours.'

Mark shook his head and laughed.

'You're better with words than me, Charlene,' he said, and my mother flinched. 'I'll admit that. But maybe some time you'll see one of my paintings.'

I didn't say a word to my mother as we left. On the drive back to Sydney Mark was very quiet, and I was afraid he was angry with me. 'No, I'm just thinking,' he said, and kissed me. As soon as we got home, he locked himself in the spare room to paint. He stayed there for almost three days, calling in sick to work. Finally he allowed me to see the finished painting. It was a portrait of my mother, with a cruel, ugly look on her face, the same look she had had on our visit. Her features were exaggerated and grotesque, and yet somehow remained remarkably close to life.

'What do you think?' Mark asked.

'It's like *The Picture of Dorian Gray*,' I said.

'If we didn't need the money I'd send it to her for her birthday,' he said. 'I'm calling it *White Australia*.'

I vowed never to speak to my mother again, unless she apologised to Mark. But with a baby on the way, and Mark giving up his job to pursue his painting, we were desperately short of money. Though Mark's work was being exhibited in several galleries, nothing had been sold yet. When our rent was six weeks overdue, I called my mother. Neither of us mentioned the visit. At first, she insisted on asking me some medical questions for one of her stories.

'What are the symptoms of meningitis?' 'If one of my characters has gout, what medicine would he take?' I patiently answered all her queries. When I began to ask for a loan, she refused at once, and said that she had to go. 'I'm busy with another collection, tell your husband. This time all the characters are as black as the ink they are written with.' I hung up.

Two days later Mark came home with a bottle of champagne. His *White Australia* had sold for almost five times its asking price in the tiny gallery in Ryde where it was being shown. The sale was even mentioned in the press, and drew attention to Mark's work. From that time, we never had to worry about money, and I was glad my mother wouldn't have the chance to refuse me again.

No publisher would take on my mother's new collection, *The Abo and Other Stories*. In the end she had to publish it herself. Mark kept clippings of all the reviews. I think he was more pleased with my mother's notices than with his own. 'Atrocious.' 'Disgusting racism.' 'Ridiculous characterisation.' 'A literary embarrassment.' Mark's favourite was in *Australian Book Review*, which said, 'I've read toilet-stall graffiti that is more creative and less offensive that Hately's latest collection.'

I went to a bookshop and bought *The Abo* and put it on the kitchen scales. It was six hundred grams, so I didn't bother to read it. My mother didn't speak to me for nine years.

THE GOOD DAUGHTER AND OTHER STORIES (SCRIBE, 2003)

From time to time I would see one of her books in the bookshop, or read her name in the newspaper. (At a creative writing conference in Launceston: 'A female writer, if she wants to be truly great, should have her tubes tied at age sixteen.') I had disappeared even from the margins of my mother's life, as I had finally disappeared from her books. And then one day, I answered the telephone and it was her.

'Hello, Barbara,' she said. 'I have an important question. It's for a story. If one of my characters has difficulty swallowing, feels fatigued and is losing weight, what might the disease be?'

I was silent.

'Well, Barbara, are you there?'

'If your character also coughed up bloody sputum, it could be lung cancer,' I said stiffly. 'That's nice and dramatic.'

'Ah. Then it seems I have lung cancer,' she said.

I drove out to see her that weekend. She was waiting for me at the door. Old age had made her a caricature of herself so that she looked more like Mark's painting than ever. As we embraced, she quavered like her pen above a blank page.

'To die of cancer,' she said. 'Christ, what a cliché. I never thought doctors actually said you had weeks to live.' She had already chosen the words on her gravestone, even the week she would die, a pessimistic month before the oncologist's estimate. (She was right.)

She made tea for us, never once mentioning my son, Michael, whom she had never seen. Instead she preferred to speak about my childhood. It was interesting to see how she had re-plotted it, working up nostalgic themes. I was conscious of every tremble on her face, as if I were watching it projected on a cinema screen. The beautiful blueness of her eyes had faded. Perhaps she had given it to too many characters. Her hands were twisted with arthritis, which she insisted was merely writer's cramp, and her skin was grey. She didn't ask me to stay, but I did, nursing her and trying to ignore her whispered asides about Mark.

At last, when she muttered something particularly vile about him, I swore and ran to my old bedroom. I threw my clothes into a bag, intending to leave her to herself. But when I kneeled to pick up a blouse from the floor, I caught sight of the edge of a picture frame tucked behind the wardrobe. There, amidst dozens of small footprints cut from novels, was Mark's painting of my mother, *White Australia*. I hid it again, then went back and told her that if she mentioned my husband again, I would leave. She nodded, white-faced, and asked me to listen to her chest. Worried, I placed the stethoscope under her nightgown.

'Your heart sounds fine,' I said.

'It's just so you know I have one,' she coughed.

In her last days she lay in bed, and I read to her. At first I tried Dickens and Hawthorne, but she said that she was sick of dead writers now that she was so soon to join them. I went to the library and borrowed some contemporary books. In between Alice Munro stories she told me, 'I have no money left after putting everything into that ... that book. There's nothing for you in the will, I'm afraid. The bank will take the house. There's hardly enough to pay for the funeral.'

I told her I didn't care, but she seemed not to hear.

'I don't regret anything, you know. Not a thing,' she went on. 'Even now there's a pen in my hand. You just can't see it. I feel sorry for you, Barbara. If you don't know how to write, then you don't know how to live.'

She told me the corrected proofs of her last collection, *The Good Daughter*, were sitting on her old desk. I went and looked. The stained glass had faded, and there was only a faint blush of colour across the pages.

As my mother was dying she quoted herself, lines from her stories, as if she wanted them to be her last words. But her last words were 'It hurts', something I heard every day that I worked in the hospital. At the end, I told her that I loved her. I don't think she understood, but the sound of the words seemed to comfort her.

The following months were strange ones for me. I felt free, and a little frightened, as a character in a story might feel if they could look past the final full stop. I sent the proofs of *The Good Daughter* to the publisher and over time they kept me informed of all the awards that it won. But I never read it, or the reviews. I was too afraid the title was ironic.

A year after my mother's death, Mark bought a copy of *The Good Daughter* and gave it to me. I read and re-read the title, then went into the kitchen and put the book on the scales.

'Well?' Mark asked.

'It's three hundred grams,' I said. 'The weight of a human heart.'

THE COCKROACH

The girl watched as the cockroach scurried over Rwanda, entirely covering the small town of Kayonza as it paused in Kibungo province. It then followed the thick, dark blue of a river to the Tanzanian border, and off the map. Crawling down the white-washed wall it settled on the floorboards in front of the bakery, where it resembled another knot in the rough wood, before disappearing into the darkness under the shop. The girl's father had laid the floorboards and carved the large wooden map that was mounted on the wall. He had let her draw in the rivers and colour the red dots of settlements, teaching her all the names at the same time. The girl liked to look at the map whenever she came to the market, though it saddened her that someone had sawn away the southwest of the country for firewood.

She was wearing her primary-school uniform, a plain blue dress. One corner of the skirt was twisted in a knot, and in the knot were her identity card and the money her father had given her to buy food. Barefoot in the mud, she turned and picked her way across the busy marketplace, ignoring the clatter of gunfire that came from a small shack showing action films on an old video recorder. In the noon sun she had to squint and the market transformed into a riot of colour. Hundreds of women in rainbow sarongs bargained and laughed under multi-coloured golfing umbrellas, while the men argued in clothes faded by the sun. On the nearby road, taxi buses with photographs of NWA or Lucky Dube taped to their windscreens idled noisily, awaiting passengers. 'Kigali! Kigali!' the convoyeurs called.

The girl walked past the men repairing bicycles, the rows of cheap digital watches, the tomatoes and onions piled into small pyramids. Carefully, she stepped between the thickening pools of blood where cows had been slaughtered that morning. Ranged around the market square were a handful of shops and bars, where the big men laughed in the shade. The girl waved to two of her cousins queuing at the water pump with their yellow dog. As she bargained for sweet potatoes, an albino knelt in front of her. He was a small, horribly sunburned man, with pink eyes, peeling lips and a raw nose. Timidly, he held out his grubby hands and whispered, 'One hundred francs. One hundred francs to eat.' The girl hesitated, then loosened the knot in her dress to give him a fifty-franc coin. The man took the money and stood.

'Cockroach!' he hissed, and spat at her.

As he limped away the girl stooped to gather some mud to throw at him. But he was already whining against the legs of some Muslims on their way to the mosque, so she let the mud slip from her fingers.

She bought the sweet potatoes, and some tomatoes and onions for lunch. Then she walked warily across the market to the shop where her father was haggling over the price of a new hammer. A man on the radio was singing a song about squashing all the cockroaches and her father listened, frowning, his eyes inflamed with sawdust. But when he saw her, he smiled. He was tall, broad and bull-necked, and he wore a pair of patched overalls that were crusted under the armpits with the salt of his dried sweat. He paid for the hammer, took the bags from her and led her away from the marketplace into the shade of the lane that led to their house. The girl walked very slowly but pretended she didn't. Her father had a limp and she knew that he didn't like her to walk ahead of him.

'You did well to get all of that for five hundred francs,' he said, looking down at her. 'What's wrong?' he asked.

'A beggar in the market called me a cockroach,' she said. 'And on the radio, on RTLM, all they talk about is killing cockroaches.'

As they walked, her father gently tapped his bad leg with the hammer, as if he could mend the badly knitted bones with it, in the same way he mended almost anything else.

'It'll be OK, you know,' he said. 'Once it was the Christians who were the cockroaches, and everyone tried to hurt them. Then for hundreds of years, it was the Jews. And now it's we Tutsi.' He winked at her. 'But when they call us cockroaches, they forget. No matter how hard you try, you can never get rid of cockroaches.' The hammer rested against his side. 'Still, I don't like all this talk either. Maybe tomorrow we'll take the bus and go to visit your uncle in Kampala. Would you like that?'

The girl nodded.

'Good, it's settled. Now, what is that there in the sky? In English.'

'A cloud,' the girl said, proud of herself.

'And in French?'

'Um ... Un nuage.'

'Excellent! And what is the date today, in French?'

'Le sixième d'Avril, dix-neuf quatre-vingt-quatorze.'

'And in English?'

'The sixth of April, nineteen ninety-four.'

They soon approached their house. The girl and her father lived in a small mudbrick hut with purple doors, overlooking the valley. The dull tin roof was warted with stones, thrown to scare away noisy crows. A workshop leaned against one wall of the house and inside were several half-finished desks and bookshelves. The shafts of light that shone through the cracks in the walls were so full of dust they seemed almost solid. When her father was busy in the workshop, he would absentmindedly stoop to avoid them.

The girl went into the bare, clean kitchen, peeled the sweet potatoes, then lit the Primus stove. Her father went into the workshop to sand some chairs. She could hear him listening to the BBC on his shortwave. Leaving the potatoes to boil, she went back outside and sat down at one of the desks with a biology book her father had bought for her. As she went from page to page the flesh dropped from the man in the book, then the muscles and the nerves, until all that was left were his bones. She turned back through the pages and clothed the skeleton once more in skin and hair. Behind her the steep hills dropped away in terraces, like steps cut for giants.

She was still sitting at the desk when her father came out of the shed. He had the radio, but it was turned down very low and she couldn't hear it properly. Standing in front of her he was very still except for the hammer that beat against his leg, so rapidly the girl thought it must hurt.

'What are they saying about the president on the news?' she asked.

Her father turned off the radio.

'Never mind that,' he said sternly. 'You know Haji?'

The girl nodded. Haji was an enormous, cheerful man who worked in the commune office. He had been a Christian before converting to Islam. Her father often joked that Haji had done so only because they had built a mosque next to his house whereas the church was ten kilometres away, on the brow of a hill. He said that if you surprised Haji he would turn Christian out of habit and call on Jesus.

Her father looked over her shoulder. The girl climbed onto the desk, shading her eyes against the sun. Down in the valley, two kilometres away, she could make out the neat, redbrick commune office. It stood at a crossroads among the fields of Irish potatoes and cassava. From all directions the girl could see pick-up trucks converging there, crowded with men standing in the trays. Her father struck the desk with the hammer and she started.

'You must listen!' he said, but when he saw that he'd frightened her he put the hammer down and went on more quietly. 'I want you to go to Haji's house now.'

'Why?'

'Because you must go. A bad thing is happening.'

They watched as the trucks stopped outside the commune office. The men jumped down and went in. When they emerged they carried in their hands things that flashed in the sun.

'Why do they have mirrors?' the girl asked.

From the office, half a dozen of the men set off across the fields to a nearby hut. They went inside, and when they came out they were laughing and dancing and the things they held didn't glint anymore. Then the girl and her father heard a truck slowly churning up the steep track that led to their house.

'They're coming,' he said. 'You must hide.'

Her father pulled her from the desk and carried her into the workshop. It was hot inside. Thick sunrays of dust fell across the clutter of tins, nails and screws, hammers, lathes and saws.

'When they leave, run to Haji's,' he said. 'He's a good friend. He'll help you get away.'

The girl laid her head on his shoulder and began to cry.

'Shh. Everyone knows you here. Go down to the border, to Tanzania. It's only sixty kilometres. It'll be fine. It'll be fine.'

The sound of the engine grew louder and her father set her down gently behind two half-finished desks.

'Come, be quiet now,' he said. 'No matter what happens, after these men leave, you go.'

'Where will we meet?' she whispered.

Her father ran his fingers down her cheek, as if feeling the grain of her skin. There was a large blue plastic tarpaulin on the floor, with the letters 'UNHCR' printed on it, and he pulled it up and covered the desks with it. Then he went outside to face them.

The girl looked through a small tear in the plastic. From her hiding place she could see them, a dozen men in ragged clothes, carrying machetes. She recognised only one of them. Augustin. He was a bald little man with bulging eyes and a wide nose. He was wearing the same grey suit that he wore to the church every Sunday. Augustin was a carpenter too, but not a very good one. His small hands were scarred and pitted and he had lost two fingertips in an accident with a chisel. He had a tight-lipped smile, as if he were holding nails in his mouth. He was smiling now. Her father stood at the doorway of the tool shed, the hammer in his hand again, tapping his knee.

'You! Fat man!' he shouted at one of the men by the truck. 'Don't touch that!'

Surprised, the man stepped back from her father's tool belt, which was hanging from a chair. But when his friends laughed at him, he turned and kicked it into the dust.

'Augustin,' her father called.

The man in the grey suit came forward. He too had a machete, which he held very carefully away from his clothes. The girl noticed it was clean. The rest were dulled and dirty.

'Wait there,' Augustin ordered the men, and they squatted around the truck.

'Where's your daughter?' Augustin asked.

'I sent her away yesterday, to Uganda,' her father replied.

'That's good,' Augustin said. 'I'm glad.'

A fly settled on his sleeve and he brushed it away.

'I've known you for thirty years, Augustin,' her father said quietly.

'I'm sorry,' the man said. 'This time ... This time they're killing all of you. Some of your Tutsi rebels, they've assassinated the president. Now the radio is saying to kill all the cockroaches.'

The men waiting by the truck took no more notice of the girl's father than of the hills or the house or the trees, and this frightened her most of all.

'It's funny, you know. You look more like a Hutu than I do,' Augustin said with his pursed smile.

'But I'm not,' her father said. Then he went on, speaking hoarsely. 'Augustin. I know what must happen. But I don't want them to cut me.'

'I understand,' Augustin said. He set the machete down on the ground, took a pistol from inside his jacket and shot her father.

As he fell he knocked over some planks leaning against the wall, coming to rest with the wood on top of him. The men cheered and didn't hear the girl cry out. She closed her eyes and for a moment more her father lived there, on her eyelids, his tall figure dark against the brightness of the square doorway. Then he was gone.

The men unloaded a crate of beer from the truck. They took it in the house and she could hear them in the kitchen, sharing out her sweet potatoes. As they ate, they sang a song:

In Heaven there's no beer,
That's why we drink it here,
When we get to Heaven,
We shall only praise the Lord.

Finally, Augustin shouted to them and they came out, spilling beer from the bottles. He wanted the men to load up the tools from the workshop, but they wouldn't listen.

'Let us see what a Tutsi woman tastes like!' they chanted, crowding into the truck. Shaking his head, Augustin climbed into the cab and the truck drove away.

Her father lay on his back, blood soaking into sawdust. She wanted to see his face but when she looked it wasn't there anymore. Turning away, she held herself for some time, sobbing. At last she got up and, facing the wall, edged slowly past the body. When she was outside she lowered her head and sprinted towards the banana plantation that covered most of the hill. There she crawled amid the thin trees, dodging the low-hanging bunches. She scrambled down the steeply sloping floor of dried brown leaves until the ground levelled. From there she could see the looping path which led to the green and white mosque. Haji lived beside it. The fields around were empty, although she could make out thin lines of smoke rising from over the hills. The girl hid on the tree line, watching, too terrified to move. She was startled at last by a crashing through the leaves beside her and she cried out, but it was only a lean, yellow dog. She recognised it as her cousins'. The dog jumped up to lick her, so she held it down by the short, ragged length of rope around its neck. Its mouth and ears were bloody.

'Shh!' she whispered, stroking the dog's back as she searched for the wound. But there was no cut or scratch on the animal. The girl shoved it away.

When the dog trotted back to her she kicked out until it ran off, barking. The girl, fearing the noise, dashed out into the open towards the mosque. She was halfway to Haji's house, where the path ran parallel with the road, when she heard a pick-up truck behind her. Turning her head she saw four whites cramped into the cab – two men and two women. They had draped a large towel over the bonnet. The girl recognised the design from school. It was the British flag. She waved to the driver, as she had always waved to whites, but he drove on without looking at her, leaving a cloud of dust.

The girl ran to the bamboo fence at the rear of Haji's cottage, slipping through a gap his goats had made. She knocked on the flaking yellow door and burst in. Haji, standing enormous in the spartan kitchen, exclaimed 'Jesus!' The girl began to cry. Haji moved slowly to her and took her in his arms.

While she told him of her father Haji led her into his small living room, with the desk and two sturdy armchairs her father had made for him. The curtains were closed and a paraffin lamp hung from a hook on the low roof. The walls were covered in newspaper to save money on paint. There were some French and English journals on one wall, but the other three were obscured by the government paper. Haji had gone over every headline and story to censor the word *inyenzi* in thick black pen. In the lamplight, the round black marks appeared to be moving, like cockroaches.

He made the girl sit down, then brought her a cup of hot, sweet tea and some bananas. 'Rest,' he said.

'Can I stay?' she asked.

He shook his head. 'The militia don't trust me. They've already searched here twice today and they'll come back. They think I'm hiding Tutsi. And now I am. You have to go, soon. I'm sorry.' When he saw her face, he added, in the official voice he usually reserved for the commune office, 'Now tell me, please.

Do you have your ID card?'

Without thinking she undid the twist of fabric in her dress and handed it to him. She watched without interest as he took the card to his desk, his wide back blocking her view. There was a Koran on the bookshelf and a small crucifix beside it on the wall. She remembered then that her father had said Haji was a large man because he contained two souls, a Christian one and a Muslim one.

The girl sat on the chair her father had made and listened to the sound of Haji typing in his slow, fore-fingered way. There was silence, then a muffled thump, a grunt, and the typing resumed. She waited. Soon Haji returned her card and told her to look at it. At first she could see nothing different. Then she realised that he had changed her tribe. He had made her a Hutu. 'I have the commune stamp with me. It looks official.' He shrugged. 'It is official. It's easy to make a forgery in a country where genuine documents look fake. It'll be good enough to get you past the roadblocks, anyway. But it won't help you here, where you're known.'

He shuffled into the kitchen and returned with a plastic bag containing a bottle of water, some sweet bread and a dozen hardboiled eggs. 'Go to Kabarondo,' he said, giving the bag to her. 'It's only eight kilometres. From there you can take a taxi bus to the border.'

Outside there was the sound of gunshots. Haji went to the window and pulled the curtain back to peer out through the dirty glass.

'Are they still showing films in the market?' the girl asked.

He nodded without turning around. Then he went to a small biscuit tin on the desk, took out a bundle of notes and placed the money in her hand. 'This is all I have,' he said. 'It'll be dark soon. You have to go out through the back fence again. Stay away from the road.'

The sound of the muezzin, distorted by static and feedback, blared from the loudspeakers of the mosque.

'They'll notice if I miss the call to prayer. Go now!' he cried and she ran, taking a narrow path that led uphill, away from her village and towards Kabarondo. Although she was used to walking six kilometres to school and back every day, she felt very tired. She saw no one as she scurried between the banana trees, eating and drinking as she went. To her surprise, she was ravenous.

After a breathless hour, when she felt she could go no farther, she saw the church. It was on top of a steep hill and she was about to sneak past when she heard the low whisper of prayers. She thought then that the priests had given sanctuary to Tutsis and she didn't have to run anymore. But as she crept closer, the whispers stopped being whispers and turned instead into a buzzing noise. The girl crawled forward, through a great hole in one corner of the church, her dress catching and tearing on a nail. The only living things inside were the flies. Above the altar, someone had placed a bloody rag over the face of the crucified Christ. She turned and fled. The sky was blood and the trees and the ground were blood as well. The sun was setting. She stumbled into the growing darkness until she tripped and fell on a hard surface, skinning her knees. It was the Kabarondo road. Before she could retreat into the bush, a voice asked, 'Where are you going?'

The girl looked up and saw a taxi bus, the words, 'Public Enmy' scratched onto the door. The convoyeur, a skinny boy, stood over her. He was smoking a cigarette, a red full stop that hung shakily near his face. She couldn't see the other passengers, for it was already too dark. The girl got up and in a faltering voice named the town on the border.

'ID card?' the boy asked, and she handed it to him. He glanced at the box that showed her ethnic group and gave the card back to her.

'How much?' she asked.

'Twelve hundred,' the boy said.

The girl handed him three five hundred franc notes. He pocketed the money but didn't give her any change. He told her to get in and she took the remaining seat, beside a drunken old man who reeked of banana wine. The convoyeur threw his cigarette away, slammed the door shut and knocked twice on the roof. The bus set off. The girl looked through her reflection in the window to the darkness beyond. No one spoke. After a while the bus slowed and stopped in the forecourt of a petrol station.

A bright light shone in her face and a voice demanded her ID card. The girl looked away. There was a felled tree across the road ahead. Some men with machetes sat on the trunk, smoking and laughing. 'Your card!' the voice repeated and she took it from her dress and held it out. The card disappeared and a lorry stopped beside the bus. In the back the girl caught a glimpse of carelessly stacked bodies, some with their insides showing like the diagrams in her biology book.

'I know this one!' a voice cried. 'Take her!' Two men dragged a pregnant woman from one of the front seats. 'She is Hutu, but she married a Tutsi!' the voice said.

The girl's ID card was thrown in her lap. Trembling, she returned it to the knot of her dress. They had to wait for the tree to be moved from the road and they could hear the woman screaming. But her silence was far worse.

'How far to the border?' the girl asked the convoyeur as they set off once more.

'Twenty kilometres,' he said.

The girl closed her eyes. For a while all she could hear was the noise of the overtaxed engine. But then she became aware of a droning behind her, and after a moment she could make out the words of a song.

'In Heaven there's no beer, that's why we drink it here,' sang a deep, slow voice. 'When we get to Heaven, we shall only praise the Lord.'

Very slowly, the girl turned round. At that instant the headlamps of a passing truck lit up the bus and she recognised Augustin sprawled across the back seats, his eyes slitted. The girl turned back quickly and tugged at the convoyeur's shirt.

'I am stopping,' she whispered. 'I am stopping here.'

The boy nodded, struck the roof once with his fist and the taxi bus came to a halt. The girl got out and without looking back walked into the grass at the side of the road. She tripped and fell over something as the bus pulled away. She didn't get up until the rear light – one was broken – had disappeared. There was a sliver of moon in the sky and almost no stars. The girl lay there until the beating of her heart stopped hurting her. Then she stood up and made her way back to the road, intending to catch the next bus that should come. She felt for the identity card. But it was gone.

She dropped to her knees and scrabbled in the dirt. Feeling all around her dress, she discovered the rip where the card must have fallen through on the bus. The girl sat on the hard ground. She remained there, unmoving, until some lights approached over a rise in the road. When they were almost upon her, she got to her feet and staggered across the furrows of a potato field. She fell again and again but kept on, away from the road, lost.

At last she came across a cattle track that wound steeply downhill through a tea plantation. She heard a rushing sound and went towards it until she found herself on the banks of a river. Exhausted, she collapsed in the long grass. She lay there for a long time. Then the water beckoned to her.

Rubbing her eyes, the girl looked again, and the water looked back. The bodies were being carried along in the strong current. Some of them seemed to be waving at her. She wondered if she would see her father there, in the water, if she waited long enough. The girl thought of him then, and of the map he had carved and fixed on the wall of the bakery. She remembered the hills he had chiselled in the wood, how he had watched her paint in the rivers and towns. And suddenly she knew the name of this river, and that it flowed down the wooden map and out over the edge, all the way to Tanzania.

The girl stood at the river's edge. When she waded in, the water was cold, but she was no longer alone. She could feel the hands of the dead holding her afloat as she swam through the darkness.

ENGLISH AS A FOREIGN LANGUAGE

'ə!' my wife says, as we make love. 'ə! ə!'

This sound, the most common in the English language, is called the schwa. It's in the last syllable of 'teacher' and the second syllable of 'understand'. It's also the noise my wife makes when she fakes an orgasm.

After a few moments, Julia groans, 'ə ə ə ə ə ...' and pushes me away from her, although I haven't yet finished. Then, reaching over, she quickly tugs an 'aʊ' (as in 'mow' and 'toe') from me with her hands. Afterwards we lie slightly apart, facing each other. My body is straight, hers arched. We resemble a child's first attempt at writing the letter b.

'Do you know what day is it tomorrow?' she asks.

'Do you know what day it is tomorrow?' I correct her.

Julia shakes her head and I close my eyes.

*

Language Focus: Listening Transcript.
'In the Classroom.'

John is teaching an English lesson. Listen carefully and answer the following questions.

1. What is the topic of the lesson?
2. Is Bob married?
3. John has forgotten something important. Can you guess what it is?

John: So, let's open our books at page 138. That's one three eight. 'Love and Marriage.' Now, let's see. Bob?

Bob: Yes?

John: Are you married?

Bob: No. I am a spinster.

John: Ha. Er ... No. A spinster is a woman. A man is a ...? Anyone?

Patrick: A bachelor.

John: Yes. Excellent. Fantastic. And Ya Mei? Are you married?

Ya Mei: No.

John: Great. And now Patrick.

Patrick: No. I am footloose and fancy-free! Like my friend Bob.

Bob: Fancy and foot? What is that?

John: I'll explain in a moment, Bob.

Patrick: John? A question, if I may?

John: Of course.

Patrick: I read somewhere that the best place to learn a foreign language is in bed. Is it true?

John: Well ... Ha, ha. Well, I think a library might be as good, as useful.

Patrick: No, I meant that having an English-speaking girlfriend is good way to learn English.

John: Ha, yes. Maybe. But ... You see, I've been married for nine years to a Hungarian and I still can't speak a word of her language!
Patrick: Nine years. Congratulations! When is your anniversary?
John: Um ... Sometime this month. It must be soon, I think. But let's move on. Ya Mei. Could you read aloud the title of the reading comprehension?
Ya Mei: 'Marriage isn't a word, it's a sentence.'
Patrick: Ha ha! That is very funny.
Bob: I don't understand. What is that?

*

As Bob and the other students leave, I clean the whiteboard, then I take my briefcase and leave the classroom. I walk down the hallway to my office, a small L-shaped room lined with grammar books and dictionaries. Taking a seat behind my desk, I open the top drawer. Beside my pencil case is a neat bundle of Julia's old love letters. Sometimes I use extracts from them in class to illustrate common mistakes. '"I very love you" isn't correct. Why?'

I take out a pen and notebook. For the last two years I have been writing an English textbook, which I hope to publish one day. There are sections on all the major skills: reading, writing, listening and speaking. This evening I'm composing a dialogue that will help students practise the many different pronunciations of the letter a.

It's this particular letter that always reminds me of the first time I met Julia, at a bar in Warsaw. I was studying my Polish phrasebook when I overheard her ordering an absinthe. Fascinated by her accent, I looked up and saw her for the first time. She seemed to be made of superlatives. She had the most beautiful face, the longest legs, the bluest eyes of any woman I had ever seen. Forgetting my shyness, I asked her where she was from and we began to converse. Occasionally, I would glance down at the topics in the phrasebook to help along my small talk. ('On Holiday' and 'My Hometown' were particularly useful.) At the end of the evening, when I asked if I could see her again, she shook her head. Seeing my disappointment, she laughed.

'I'm from Hungary, remember,' she said. 'In Hungary, nodding head means no, and shaking head means yes.'

Later, after we slept together for the first time, I asked her why she had bothered with me that night, awkward as I was. 'Because you were the only man in that room more interested in my a's than my ass,' she said.

'A,' I write now, and then spend an hour formulating pronunciation exercises. After that, I turn to another topic; one that most textbooks choose to ignore. Under the heading 'Bad Language' I have compiled a list of swear words and calculated their offensiveness with a rating from + to ++++. The first entry is '"Ass" (US English) and "Arse" (British English) ++.' I make a note to later expand and explain 'Kiss my ass,' 'You bet your ass,' and 'To kick someone's arse.' On consideration, I also decide to upgrade 'cock' to +++. Then I notice that it's late. When I call home, Julia says carefully, 'Do you know what day *it is?*'

'It's Wednesday.'

'It's our wedding anniversary.'

When I try to apologise she calls me a word (rated ++++ on my list) and hangs up.

By the time I get home, Julia has already gone upstairs. She is lying asleep on the bed, naked, as is her habit. On her left breast she has written, in black paint, 'Call', and on the other breast, 'Patrick'.

Years ago, Julia grew tired of how I always missed the messages she took down when I was out. She began to write them on her body, knowing that I would see them when I got home. Sometimes when I came back late I'd wake her with the touch of the paintbrush, correcting the mistakes. And then we would make love.

It's been a long time since my wife has made any mistakes in her writing.

*

LANGUAGE FOCUS: PHONETIC SCRIPT.

The International Phonetic Alphabet (IPA) is a system of symbols based on the Latin alphabet, representing the spoken sounds of language. For example, the first line of Hamlet's famous soliloquy is rendered thus in phonetic script:

/tə biː ɔːr nɒt tə biː ðæt ɪz ðə ˈkwestʃən/

The IPA can be an extremely useful tool for English learners as it can help them pronounce new vocabulary correctly, and can mark the stress on unfamiliar words.

Exercise: Change the following sentences from phonetic script to standard English. The first has been done for you.

1. /ˈlæŋgwɪdʒ ɪz ðə sɔːs əv ˌmɪsʌndəˈstændɪŋz/

Language is the source of misunderstandings.

2. /wɜːds ɑːr ðə fiːˈzɪʃənz əv ə dɪˈziːzd maɪnd/

3. /dʒuːlɪʌ ɪz fʌkɪŋ pætrɪk/

*

Patrick is Rwandan. He has a narrow nose, large, round eyes and three short scars like the arms of a capital E on his right cheek. I envy him all this. In comparison I'm quite adjectiveless. His English is excellent, though his preference for the longer forms of tenses – 'I am' instead of 'I'm' and 'It is' instead of 'It's' – can make him sound overly formal. Whenever I tell him this he chuckles, saying, 'I want to have as few contractions as a peasant giving birth in the fields.'

Patrick was one of my first students. I taught him when he was in Elementary. In our second lesson I asked the class to draw their family tree. Patrick wrote only his own name in the middle of the paper and, thinking he hadn't understood, I explained the instructions again.

'No, I understand,' he said. 'That is me. I am the family tree.'

For the first two years I knew him, this was the only reference he made to the genocide. But when he advanced to Academic, he began to write essays and make presentations on Rwanda. This was the one topic that he would never get full marks for, because he would write and speak only in clichés.

'All of my family and all my friends are gone,' he would say. 'They are as dead as a dodo, as dead as a doornail. But I was slippery as a snake. I hid in a pit latrine for six days. Not enough room to swing a cat and it smelled to high heaven. But on the seventh day I climbed out of there like a monkey. Believe me, I didn't smell of roses, and I was hungry enough to eat a horse.'

Finally, I asked him if he spoke of Rwanda like this because it was too painful to talk about directly. But Patrick only smiled and said, 'You took the words right out of my mouth.'

Although his English is almost perfect, he insists we continue to meet for private lessons. At first we had them at home

33

but Julia objected, and so for an hour every week the two of us walk along the harbour, pausing often, like the fingers of a slow reader across a page. If the conversation lulls, Patrick mutters 'Red lorry, yellow lorry' under his breath, for like all Rwandans, he has trouble distinguishing between r and l. He likes to look at the women we pass; sometimes I have to remind him that staring is rude in Australia.

'There is no word for "stare" in Kinyarwanda,' he says sadly. Then he smiles and claps his hands. 'Anyway, let us revise making plans. Present continuous for the future, yes?'

I nod.

'What are you doing tomorrow?' he asks.

'I'm teaching.'

'Really? When are you teaching?'

'From eight till five. What—'

'Can I ask the questions, please?' he grins. 'It is good revision. As I was saying ... What are you doing after teaching?'

'I'm correcting homework for a couple of hours.'

'Around around the ragged rock, the ragged rascal ran,' Patrick says thoughtfully.

*

Language Focus: Predictions using 'will' and 'going to'.

Exercise: Before reading the rest of the text complete the following:

1. I think Patrick is going to ....

2. Perhaps John will ....

3. It's likely Julia is going to ....

*

At five o'clock, when the last of the students leave, I'm on the way to my office to do some marking. Then I think of Julia. I decide to go home early for the first time in many weeks.

It's a warm evening and I take a shortcut, walking down a long street flanked by garages. Sometimes I like to come here and puzzle out the grammar of the graffiti. There's a white car similar to my own parked on the other side of the road. As I walk past I glance at the registration and see that it is my car. I make out the profile of a man in the passenger window.

'Hey!' I shout as I cross the street. 'What are you fucking doing in my car?'

Startled, the man turns to face me. It's Patrick. His shocked expression is almost comical, as if he were miming the word 'surprise' in class. Looking through the window I can make out a woman's head resting on his lap.

'Patrick?' I say. 'What are you doing fucking in my car?'

The woman looks up. It's Julia.

*

35

LANGUAGE FOCUS: VOCABULARY.

Study this vocabulary list of the ninth year of John and Julia's marriage. Look up any unfamiliar words in the dictionary.

chore	missionary
grind	mortgage
ennui	utilities
tunnel	routine
peccadilloes	defenestration

*

Obviously, at the end of the day, I'm absolutely devastated. I stagger away from the car like a drunk, crying like a baby. Julia is calling my name, but I pretend to be deaf as a post. I'm reeling from the news, and in denial. I never knew my wife could be so two-faced. And Patrick. Maybe it was all a dream, I tell myself. But no, it's as plain as the nose on my face. The night is still young, so I keep walking until I find a bar. I order an ice-cold bottle of beer and gulp it down. Then I have another and another until I'm drunk as a skunk. Standing at a table nearby there is a big man with bulging biceps. On his left arm is tattooed the words 'Australias Own'. I take a pen from my jacket pocket and, quiet as a church mouse, sneak up beside him and add an apostrophe to make 'Australia's'. Quick as a flash, I am lying on the floor, seeing stars. My nose is broken and I'm bleeding like a stuck pig. The man kicks me on the side of the head and I go out like a light.

*

Language focus: Word Search.

Exercise: Test your knowledge of English by finding six words below relating to the future of John and Julia's marriage. The first has been done for you.

f	q	r	y	u	i	p	l	k	r
b	a	b	y	m	n	b	c	y	e
x	c	d	a	g	l	u	c	g	c
z	c	b	p	o	i	n	u	t	o
s	e	p	a	r	a	t	i	o	n
r	e	w	q	n	l	k	j	h	c
f	o	r	g	i	v	e	n	f	i
p	l	e	m	n	g	r	d	x	l
z	r	b	y	h	j	k	d	q	e
p	s	s	e	n	i	p	p	a	h

*

When I wake up in the hospital, my wife is sitting beside the bed. Julia is no longer made of superlatives, but comparatives. She is less beautiful than before, her eyes are redder, and she seems much older.

With the cast on my leg, and the bandages wrapped round my head, I must resemble a picture from the chapter on 'Health' in my textbook. In fact, Julia's first words to me are exactly the same as in a dialogue I wrote last week, 'In Hospital'.

'What happened?' she says. 'You look terrible.'

I'm about to reply, 'You should see the other guy,' but instead I follow the script and say, 'I had an accident.'

I remember when I first started the school, and I couldn't afford the tapes that went with the textbooks. Julia and I would record the dialogues together. I was the train conductor, the postman, the lost tourist and she was the wife, the reception-ist, the chef. We used to laugh so much that it would take us hours to record a few lines. We were happy. But when the stu-dents complained that Julia's accent was too difficult to follow, I recorded over her. The dialogues became monologues.

'The doctor said that your ankle is broke,' Julia says and for once, I don't correct her. 'And your nose. Also, three of your ribs, and you have a serious concussion. You could have died.'

'How long have you been seeing him?' I ask, grateful for pro-nouns so I don't have to say Patrick's name.

'It only started last month,' Julia says. 'He came round one day when you were at the school. There was that time, and the time ... Last night. I have no excuse. It's just that I didn't feel like I was married anymore. Words were more important to you than marriage.'

'Marriage isn't a word,' I whisper, my throat dry. 'It's a sentence.'

Julia raises a glass of water to my mouth, and I drink.

'John,' she says. 'You know ... This was ... I can't ...' and then, without realising it, she begins to talk in Hungarian. I listen to her, nodding and smiling slightly, as my own students do when they don't understand me. Julia's voice sounds younger.

I never realised how beautiful her language is. Soon, she is crying. It's the first time I have seen her cry. Perhaps she couldn't in English. As she goes on, it seems to me that I understand everything she says. Finally, I raise my right hand a couple of inches from the bed. It trembles as if I were a nervous student wanting to ask a question. She stops speaking and looks at me.

'Julia,' I say. 'I'm sorry. I'm so sorry.'

She is silent.

'I love you,' I say, and still she says nothing. My hand remains raised. There is one question I have to ask. 'Do you still love me?'

Julia looks at me for a long time. Then she shakes her head.

AFRICA WAS CHILDREN CRYING

Gilchrist was awakened by a caress. Squinting into the sunlight he saw the scabbed stump of a beggar's arm stroking his cheek through the glassless window of the bus.

'Jesus!' he cried in disgust. He thrust the mutilation away from his sunburned face, as the trussed chickens at his heels rioted. 'Christ,' he muttered, wiping his cheek. 'Jesus Christ.'

The beggar had fallen back into the dirt and dried dung of the roadside. He sat there patiently, his half-arm raised like a conductor's baton. A fat woman, cramped in beside Gilchrist, said, 'Ah, my friend, that is Africa.'

She waved the beggar off, saying something in dialect, but he wouldn't move. Remembering Elizabeth, Gilchrist squirmed a hand into his pocket to pick out a coin. But his wedding ring caught on his belt and then the bus jolted into motion. The beggar stood and followed in a limping run, his hand gripping Gilchrist's forearm as the bus gathered speed. With his free hand Gilchrist tried to prise the beggar's away.

'For God's sake! Let go!' he shouted, and threw out the window the first thing he could find, a golden chocolate-bar wrapper. It spun in the wind before settling by a cow herder asleep on the side of the road. The beggar sprinted towards the herder and his cattle, his fist flourishing a rock, screaming until he drove them away. He found the golden wrapper, burnished into beauty by the sun, and held it up as if looking for the watermark in some strange currency.

Gilchrist turned away with relief, his knees aching against the torn fabric of the seat in front. He was a tall man, and the sun had marked borders of pink on his arms and neck. He spat on his hand to wipe his face once more, but the saliva was red from the dust blown through the broken window. Africa was in his lungs. In distant fields he could see faint human figures halving and doubling in size with the rise and fall of hoes. The sun fixed everything with a long shadow. Some cows lay in the sparse shade of matoke trees, their tails winnowing the dry air above their bony shanks. The bus was overcrowded, almost thirty passengers, including children, when it had been built for only fifteen. Strangers held each other or sat on each other's laps in innocent intimacy. Gilchrist felt his fat neighbour's perspiration soaking into his side so that any movement he made seemed almost sexual. He could tell she was wealthy, as her hair was braided into an intricate spiral, speared with a short length of ivory so she could scratch her scalp through the patterns. Behind the driver three nuns sang alien hymns out of which a nasal Christ occasionally showed Himself.

Gilchrist reached into his pocket for his wallet and took out a photograph. He had only this one picture of his wife, the others having been stolen from a bag in Nairobi. It was taken a week after their third miscarriage. Elizabeth was standing in front of the Opera House, one hand resting on her stomach, feeling for kicks that would never come. It was that day, he remembered now, she had suggested they go travelling together. Gilchrist

41

had agreed, as long, he said, as they were travelling to get to a place and not simply to leave one.

'Do you think I want to travel just to leave Sydney?' she asked.

'No. To leave the empty nursery.'

'I can't get away from that,' she said. 'I carry it with me.'

The Ugandan woman beside him took the photograph from his hands. 'Who is the lady?' she asked.

'It's my wife,' Gilchrist answered.

'She is very beautiful,' the woman said. 'You must love her and miss her. You have children?'

'No,' Gilchrist said. 'One day. My wife loves children.'

'Then she must love Africa because Africa is children.'

'Yes, she loves Africa.' Gilchrist would have been happy to leave after a week, to go on to South America, but Elizabeth wanted to visit orphanages and help the children. Gilchrist refused to go again after their first orphanage visit, which had depressed him a great deal. 'We give money,' he had said. 'What else can we do?' It was then she had insisted on going to see the gorillas alone. Like a child, Gilchrist had hoped he would become sick, so she would have to stay and look after him. But she had gone.

'She will be a good mother and you a good father,' the Ugandan woman said. 'Where is this picture made? America? England?'

'No. Australia.'

'You are Australia?'

'Yes,' he said, not bothering to correct her. 'From Sydney.'

'Ah, Sydney.'

Wistfully, the woman looked past him out the window, as if expecting the Harbour Bridge to rise from the fields. 'Where is she now, your wife?'

'She went to visit the gorillas.'

'Yes, the Mountains of the Moon! You did not go with her?'

'No.'

'Why not?'

'Could I have my photograph, please?' Gilchrist asked.

'Here.' She turned her enormous smile to him. 'Perhaps we can correspond?'

'Fine,' Gilchrist said bleakly. He had lost count of the times these last months he had been asked for a scholarship, a pen pal, a job at the Australian embassy. He tore a page from the novel he was reading and wrote in the margin, 'Charles Chaplin, 221b Baker Street, Brigadoon, Tasmania.' The woman beamed at him over her three chins. Gilchrist hid his face in the book. His neighbour read over his shoulder for some time, then dozed off.

The bus, painted with rust and orange mud, climbed steeply for an hour, bucking in the rain ruts that scored the ground. Then it came to a stop at a roadblock, a dead tree administered by three policemen playing cards on the trunk. Behind them a line of women and children stood on the edge of the road before it became nothing. Not far away a boy was weeping beside two split-open cows, the flies settling on his face to drink from his tears. Around his feet, fragments of broken glass shone.

The woman beside Gilchrist said 'A crash,' and crossed herself. The passengers disembarked in silence. The fat woman went to speak to one of the policemen. Gilchrist tried not to think that all African languages sounded the same. 'A bus and cows together,' the woman called to Gilchrist. 'It has fallen down the hill. Many hurt, many dead. Many Africa and a Europe.' She waved at him. 'My home is here. I am stopping here. Goodbye.'

'Goodbye,' Gilchrist said. He presented his worn passport to a policeman and tried to stretch the stiffness from his limbs.

The fat woman had joined the crowd at the cliff edge. She shouted to Gilchrist, 'Look. Come. Look.' But the sight of the cows had made him ill, and he had no desire to see the wreck. Already he could imagine the accident as something he would tell Elizabeth. He would describe the dead cows and how they had upset him, and she would comfort him. He turned to get back on the bus, but the woman rushed over and seized his arm. She held him as she spoke excitedly to the policeman in dialect, delving into her enormous bag to fetch the page where he had written the false name and address. Gilchrist imagined there must be some problem with her papers and she was using him to explain it away.

'What's she saying?' he asked the policeman. 'I don't know her. She's nothing to me.'

He was afraid of complications if the policeman compared the false name he had given her with his passport. Gilchrist shook the woman's hand from his forearm. As if she couldn't maintain her balance she took the policeman's elbow, arguing with him and pointing as they unloaded bags of fruit from the back of the bus. One of the bags split open and the tomatoes rolled around the dead cows like great atoms of blood. The bored expression on the faces of the policemen didn't waver and they pushed her away. 'Wait!' she cried to Gilchrist. 'Please!'

Ignoring her, he climbed back into the bus and sat beside an elderly man who was reading a month-old *London Times*. The bus set off immediately. As the sunlight shone full upon him through the broken window, Gilchrist began to shiver. He knew it was malaria. A month earlier he had lain sleepless and feverish for days in a Nairobi hotel room while Elizabeth had nursed him, almost gratefully, he thought. She never loved him more than when he was sick. Then she could feel like a mother. Fort Portal, where they were to meet in four days, was still hours away. Gilchrist looked at the sun, which divided itself like a fertilised cell. In its light the horizon quavered and banked. The driver swerved and jerked through potholes, cursing at the filthy lorries transporting cargo to the coast. The passengers trampolined joylessly in their hard, patched seats. Gilchrist squirmed and swallowed his nausea while a baby cried and cried, as if for future sorrow.

'Excuse me, is the road as bad as this all the way to Fort Portal?' he asked the old man.

'*Non.* It improves very much, *c'est très bien*, near Nyabagogo, where the Chinese are building a new road. Are you British or *Français?*'

'Tell me – how far is Nyabagogo?' Gilchrist asked.

'Sixty kilometres,' the old man said brightly, 'and until then, all uphill and downhill. Look at these peasants here ...' He nodded at two women in the next row. 'Watch them when we go down the hills. Eh, my friend! Then you will see vomiting!' The old man appeared proud of this, as if it were a natural feature of his country no tourist should miss. 'I can speak several languages,' he told Gilchrist earnestly. 'Please, do you know of how I can gain employment with the UN?'

'I'm sorry,' Gilchrist said.

The old man solemnly shook his hand and went back to the *Times*.

Soon after, when a truck had nearly murdered them all on a blind corner, Gilchrist could no longer endure it. He had the bus stop in a dry valley, where steep, tree-choked hills surrounded a village of a dozen houses. There were perhaps more dwellings than he thought – he still couldn't differentiate between a house and a goat shed. But he had glimpsed a hotel-sign leaning against one of the larger adobe buildings. He paid the driver more than his guidebook advised, too unwell to argue, and was left with his rucksack by the rusted frame of a pram. The bus drove away, its shadow hiding underneath it as if itself seeking shade. Gilchrist read the clumsily painted sign resting against the mud wall: 'Hotel Wellcome'. Underneath was painted a perspectiveless bed and a yellow roast chicken with wavy lines of aroma radiating from it.

Gilchrist dragged his luggage through a dark, crooked doorway. Inside, there was a counter cobbled from cardboard boxes and plywood, behind which a small, very dark man sat on an upturned beer crate. He was reading a book with no cover and at his back, secured with huge nails that had cratered the wall, was a large children's map of the world. A spotted pink stain overspread Africa like a sickly new Empire.

'Hello. I would like a room please,' Gilchrist said in his grammar-book English.

'Certainly. You are welcome,' the man replied, his softly accented voice somewhat difficult to understand. Then Gilchrist noticed the harelip, which formed a delta on the left of his mouth.

'I am Abraham,' the man said.

'I am Gilchrist. I mean, John,' Gilchrist said. They shook hands.

'It is a pleasure to meet you. Follow me, please.'

Pulling aside a curtain, Abraham created a rectangle of light in the back wall. Gilchrist left his rucksack and followed him outside. The late-afternoon sunlight had the weight and texture of tepid water on his skin and his legs trembled. They stood in an irregular courtyard of brown dirt, swept into symmetrical swirls. On three sides of the square were ranged several small rooms, numbered randomly from twenty to three hundred. Washing lines, bent with drying clothes, crossed the yard. In one corner an old woman was bathing a sleepy baby boy in a plastic basin. She looked up at Gilchrist and smiled. Somewhere, children were playing.

'The room,' Abraham said. Gilchrist gratefully stepped out of the sun into the cramped space, which was at least clean and boasted a mosquito net fixed above the hard single bed. Wedged in beside it was a bow-legged table, and an erratic line of coat hooks ascended one of the green walls. The only window, covered by mended mosquito netting, was near the door and faced into the courtyard.

'Fine,' Gilchrist said, sitting down. 'I don't suppose there is a doctor in town?'

'Town? Do you mean here? No, there is no doctor. Are you ill?'

'Malaria. It's fine. I've had it before and I have the drugs for it. All I need is some water, and the bathroom.'

'Malaria, yes, I myself have had it for some three days now. I'll bring you water immediately. The bathroom is across there,' Abraham said, pointing across the courtyard. Then Gilchrist was left alone. He lay down for a few moments, then stood unsteadily and went out into the heat. He paced slowly across the compound to the pit latrine, like a pirate measuring out his treasure. Breathing though his mouth, he urinated over the flies that flew up, dazed and bloated, from the hole. Outside, he washed his hands under the warm drip of a broken tap. The baby was being dried off after his bath. Drops of water curved and traced along the child's perfect brown skin and his eyes were astonished. Gilchrist reached to take his small hand but the baby writhed away, howling. The old woman hushed him and began to sing.

Gilchrist returned to his room. On the table Abraham had left a warm bottle of water and a plastic tumbler, and his rucksack was by the bed. He undressed and lay down. Slow lines of perspiration sneaked across the sunburned border on his neck and arms. The inside of his skin felt bruised and he believed he could hear the pupils in his eyes whirring like camera lenses. In the courtyard the baby was still coughing out his cries over the woman's lullaby. Gilchrist felt the fever upon him. He gulped down two of the malaria pills with the warm water and fell asleep.

All at once he started awake as an artillery shell ricocheted off the door. Giggling, scuffling noises filled the air amidst whoops and shouts, worrying the baby into a baroque pattern of bawling. A ragged ball made from plastic bags hit the window, shuddering the cloudy glass. Gilchrist closed his eyes again, wincing from time to time at the shrieking outside. At dusk Abraham brought some more water, a plate of beans and a copy of yesterday's English-language newspaper, the *New Vision*. He stood with his head bowed while Gilchrist drank and retrieved the untouched plate without comment.

Gilchrist said, 'I can hear children. Are they yours?'

'Yes,' Abraham answered proudly. 'I have four. The baby, who is not named yet. Then there is Garçon, the boy, and Girl. And Ruth the older, who is ten.'

'Ruth? That's a lovely name.'

Gilchrist and Elizabeth had long ago chosen Ruth for a girl's name and John for a boy. John was Gilchrist's name. After the last miscarriage his wife used it less and less, instead calling him 'darling' or 'dearest'. His name had died with the child in the womb. Even for him. He thought of himself as Gilchrist now.

'There are only four of them? I thought there were more,' Gilchrist smiled.

'They have been disturbing you?' the small man frowned and at once his harelip became a duelling scar.

'No, no. Please just ask them to play somewhere else,' Gilchrist said. 'There is a whole continent after all.'

That night he lay muttering in the dark, under the mosquito net. He noosed the bed sheets around his sweating back until dawn came and, disbelieving in sleep, he fell asleep.

He was awoken twenty minutes later. It was six o'clock in the morning. He arose weakly outraged, as if disturbed from his deathbed. Yanking open the door, he found Abraham's four children in the courtyard. A boy of eight or nine was drumming a rock on the dented bottom of a powdered milk tin. Behind him his taller sister danced in the remains of a wedding dress, her little stomach distended with worms so that she seemed grotesquely pregnant. A small girl carried the grizzling baby on her back, held in place by a bright yellow shawl. She was drawing pictures in the dirt with a pointed stick, trying to interest the child. Gilchrist struggled to recall their names. He called out softly, 'Garçon. Ruth.'

Garçon looked up at Gilchrist and gave a scream that almost felled the sick man. The boy fled and his little sister followed with the baby. They had jilted Ruth, the girl in the dirty lace, who caught her feet in her train and tripped over. When Gilchrist, grinning wanly, took a step towards her, she howled and wet herself. He turned away in disgust and slammed the door. Through the window, in dirty sepia, he saw Garçon return to drag his sister away.

'Run, run,' Gilchrist whispered. 'Good practice for when you're refugees.'

He sat in bed all day trying to read the newspaper. Abraham left his food and water at the door. Gilchrist couldn't find the World Service on his clockwork radio and winding it left him exhausted. At night he lay naked on the bed, flushed with the parasites bursting in his liver. He closed his eyes but couldn't sleep. As the sun rose he took his pills and drank some water, which appeared to fill his bladder instantly. After enduring the discomfort for half an hour he danced awkwardly into his trousers to go and relieve himself. He nearly fainted in the latrine and rushed out, terrified he was about to fall, Alice-like, down the hole.

Seeing something white dash from his doorway, he grabbed at it, lost his balance and almost fell. His left hand held a girl's wrist. It was Ruth, the child bride, her eyes a caricature of terror.

'What were you doing in my room?' Gilchrist said furiously.

Ruth wailed something, her other hand behind her back.

'Let me see,' Gilchrist said. She tried to twist away from him and in the struggle, she let something drop to the step. It was his photograph of Elizabeth. When the girl had torn it from his wallet it had ripped almost in two, and now only a crease of shiny skin held it together. Gilchrist squeezed her wrist. Why was this Ruth alive, he wondered, when theirs had died? The girl scratched his arm. Gilchrist slapped her once on the cheek with the back of his hand. Blood welled from a cut in her lip where his wedding ring had caught her. He let go and she ran off into the darkness. Gilchrist looked around the empty compound, then went inside.

At eight in the morning, half-dressed and barely conscious, he became aware of a swishing sound followed by hysterical yowling. He struggled to the door against the heaving deck of the ground and, opening it, saw Abraham beating his daughter with a long piece of bamboo. Ruth writhed in his grip, unable to wriggle out of the scrap of lace he held her by. As the cane descended she yelped and yelled, reminding Gilchrist of a goat he had seen slaughtered in a Freetown market. He staggered out into the overexposed air.

'Abraham, what's happened?' he said.

Abraham stopped. Ruth circled her father, tethered as by a rope to his arm.

'I am beating her because she has deceived me,' Abraham said. 'Look here, sir,' and he pulled the child forward without effort even as she grooved trenches with her heels in the dry earth. Ruth's lips were swollen and her wrist bruised.

'She says that the white man – pardon me, sir, but that is what she said – she said that you did this. And I know she must be deceiving me, so I am punishing her. She is deceiving us, sir, yes?'

'Yes,' Gilchrist said.

Then he lurched past them and was sick in the pit latrine. When he emerged, the child was still being beaten, the bamboo falling a dozen more times to meet its shadow on her back.

'She will not be a deceiver, and neither will the others!' Abraham bellowed over the child's squeals. 'Look, they are seeing.' With his bamboo switch, he gestured at one of the eccentrically numbered rooms. On a step, watching, were Ruth's brothers and sister. The baby boy, held in the smallest child's arms, sucked undisturbed at a plastic doll's leg. The beaten child began to wail again.

'She must stay out here, for punishment,' Abraham said as he hit the girl once more, across the thighs. He left her there, snivelling and shaking.

Gilchrist turned his back on the children and locked the door of his room. He pulled covers and clothes over himself. The girl's moaning continued in the courtyard outside for a quarter of an hour, broken sometimes by a raw hiccough. The monotony of her distress maddened him. Finally, Gilchrist mimicked the child's groaning, quietly at first, then, throwing his covers away, he echoed her louder and louder until Ruth realised she was being mocked. She began to scream out in spluttering frustration, 'Imana weh! Yesu weh! Mfasha!'

Gilchrist knew enough of the language to know that she was calling to God. He parroted the spat syllables awkwardly, again and again, until at last the child and the man halted together. Then there was only the sound of his laboured breathing. He fell asleep.

After twelve hours he woke and the fever had left him. He was upset to find he had destroyed Elizabeth's picture as he slept. Resting in bed he tried to gentle out the creases with his fingers, but it was ruined. There was no sound of the children all that morning.

At lunchtime he got up and packed his things. He found Abraham sitting behind his makeshift desk, listening to the static-cracked English of the radio.

'You have recovered!' he said.

'Almost,' Gilchrist replied, counting out the money he owed. 'I still feel weak. Could you tell me when the next bus to Fort Portal will pass by?'

'In about forty minutes.'

Gilchrist thanked him and went to sit on the hotel's front steps to await the bus. The children peered out at him from the corner of the building and when he ignored them, came round. They gathered together in a little convocation and whispered, as if they feared he could understand them. Ruth stood smirking shyly at him. Gilchrist threw them some money, more than he had paid their father for his stay. While they fought over the notes he crossed the road and walked as far away from the hotel as he could. He waited in the shade, reading and watching the peasants at work in the banana fields.

The bus was an hour late. He felt profound relief when he saw the steering wheel covered in pink fur and the two pictures stuck to the windscreen, one of Jesus, the other of Sylvester Stallone. Gilchrist took the last seat and they set off. In the rear-view mirror he saw a pillar of dust blot out the settlement. The four hours to Fort Portal passed quickly after they reached the new tarmac road.

Fort Portal was one of the larger, more developed towns, though Gilchrist would never have known this but for the guidebook. He got off the bus and went along a mud road sculpted by rains. Some schoolchildren followed him, whispering incorrect French greetings punctuated by the flip-flop of their sandals. Their small dark faces were beautiful above the bright blue of their uniforms. In the market square the ground stank with dried cow blood and old women raked up fruit skins, plantain stalks and horns to bonfire along the road. Gilchrist soon found the hotel where he was to meet Elizabeth. She wasn't there, although she should have arrived the previous day. He bought a *New Vision* and walked slowly across the square (his joints still ached) to a small restaurant and had rice and beans and some UHT milk. Opening the newspaper, he drank the last drops of the milk, which were like baby teeth at the bottom of the tin mug. Four schoolchildren lingered outside to stare at him.

'Hello,' he said.

'Hello,' they giggled.

'How are you?'

'How are you?' they repeated. Gilchrist waved and started to read his newspaper. On the third page, beside an advertisement for margarine, there was an article about a bus that had crashed four days before on a mountain pass sixty-five kilometres from Nyabagogo. Twenty people had been killed. The authorities had just released their names. Third from the top, he saw his own.

'Oh God,' he cried. 'Oh Jesus. Help me.'

And a part of him heard the schoolchildren cheerfully sing as one, 'Ohgod ohjesus helpme! Ohgod ohjesus helpme!'

FOUR LETTER WORDS

Cock

My father was very fond of telling the story of how he first met my mother because of a cock. He would always begin the same way, explaining that he had been born in Scotland (though this was obvious enough from his accent) in a village near Aberdeen. He had come to Australia at the age of twenty-five and settled in Newcastle because it had the same name as the English city. After some odd jobs, he found work as an apprentice glazier.

One day my father was sent to a property in Bar Beach. The owner was a wealthy lawyer who kept a large greenhouse, chicken coop and vegetable garden, which he liked to potter around in on weekends. My father was to replace several panes in the greenhouse, which had been damaged in a storm. While he worked, the owner tried to chat with my father about his prize chickens, but when he couldn't understand my father's replies he eventually went back inside. My father took this opportunity to have a cigarette break. As he leaned against the fence, smoking, the latch gave way behind him and a rooster scarpered out of the coop. Closing the gate, my father chased after the rooster, which ran down the driveway towards the ocean. My father dove at it, but the bird flapped in the air and over a high wall into the garden of the house next door. Pulling himself over the wall, my father landed a few inches from my mother, a 22-year-old girl, sunbathing in her underwear while her parents were away for the day.

Out of breath, he panted, 'Excuse me, Miss. Have you seen my cock?'

This word, derived from the Old English *cocc*, is commonly used in Scotland to describe a male domestic fowl. My mother didn't know this. She screamed and slapped my father in the face so hard that she bloodied his nose. At that moment the rooster came squawking from the open door of the house and my father was able to catch it. He held the struggling bird with one hand and his streaming nose with the other. My mother, realising that he wasn't a pervert after all, went to fetch a handkerchief. While she was gone, my father spotted a crack in one of the lounge-room windows. When my mother returned with the hankie, he pointed it out. Fearing her parents would notice the damage, my mother became upset, until my father explained his trade and offered to repair the window free of charge. That afternoon, he asked my mother out. They were married two years later.

FART

When I was a small boy, my father taught me his national anthem, 'Scotland the Brave'. My mother loved to hear me sing it, especially the first verse:

Land of my high endeavour
Land of the shining river
Land of my heart forever
Scotland the brave!

Whenever her relatives visited (which wasn't often, as they never liked my father), she would have me stand on a chair and sing; my father would accompany me on the mouth organ. Shortly before my grandparents came one day, my father took me aside, explaining he hadn't taught me the first verse properly. Together we rehearsed the new words:

Fart, fart, my bum is calling,
Must be the beans I ate this morning,
Quick, quick, the lavvy door,
Too late, it's on the floor.

After my grandparents arrived, my mother, as usual, requested me to sing 'Scotland the Brave'. I never reached the second verse. At the end of the first, I was snatched from the chair as my father, bent double with laughter, spat his harmonica across the kitchen. My mother took me to my room and spanked me with the *Macquarie Dictionary*, to teach me not to say bad words. She was both angry and embarrassed. (My mother's face never showed one emotion, but always a mixture of two, like a portmanteau word.) At bedtime, my father crept into the room with a smuggled lollipop. Flicking through the *Macquarie*, he said, 'This isn't a proper dictionary. It doesn't have any of the best words.'

He took a pen and wrote 'Fart' after 'Farrow' with the definition, 'To produce a bad smell from the bottom.' (I informed him much later that 'fart' is one of the oldest English words, with many cognates in other languages.)

My father found flatulence hilarious. One of his favourite tricks was to have pie and beans for lunch at work, then return home and close all the windows and doors in the living room. For twenty minutes he would sit and break wind, only then calling my mother in from the kitchen. 'Oh, Jimmy!' she would shout, and he would laugh as she ran, retching, from the room. He always boasted of his complete control of his bowels and would challenge me to say 'When,' at which point he would instantly fart. Sometimes I would wait for hours, then cry, 'When!' and he would let out a loud one. My mother, when she heard him, would shake her head in disgust and run around the house, opening all the windows.

I wasn't allowed to say 'fart', so my father taught me the Doric for it, *braim*. Doric was the dialect of Aberdeenshire, where my father grew up. Even as a child I was fascinated by the different sounds and meanings the words had, and I began to realise, dimly, that language was shaped by place. By the age of four I could talk with my father in dialect, and my mother would have no idea what we said.

My father rarely swore at home. Sometimes if he was talking about his employers he would say, 'They're a shower of bastards, the lot of them,' and my mother would shoosh him. It was difficult to catch him swearing because his accent seemed to make even the mildest words profanities.

Once, my mother and I glued together a little cardboard box and cut a slit at the top. This was the swear box, and my father had to put in twenty cents every time he cursed. My mother made the mistake of promising me the money from the box when it was full, so I used to provoke my father. The easiest way to do this was to break wind myself. Most of the time I wasn't able to and just gave myself stomach cramps, but when I did my father would cry out in amusement, 'Was that you, you dirty wee bastard?'

And twenty cents would go in the box.

POOF

At the time I started school, I had a pronounced lisp that my mother blamed on the strange sounds I had made when speaking Doric with my father. She was very worried about this, but my father insisted I would grow out of it, as I did, in fact, a year or two later. But in my first week in kindergarten, an older boy caught me in the playground and, calling me a 'Poof,' punched me in the face. I ran back to our house with a split lip. My father came home to find me sobbing in the bathroom as my mother dabbed cotton wool on the cut.

'What happened, son?' he said, putting down his newspaper.

'Have you been drinking?' my mother asked him, but my father ignored her.

I told him what the boy had done, which seemed to me the most serious part, and only as an afterthought what he had called me.

'Fucking bastard,' my father said quietly. 'Little fucking bastard! Calling my son a poof? No one calls my son a poof!'

'Jimmy!' my mother cried.

He went out through the kitchen to the shed and returned a minute later holding a hammer.

'What's his name?' he asked me.

'Stelio Grivas.'

'A fucking wog, is he? We'll see what his father has to say about it. Come on.'

'Jimmy, don't,' my mother said, clutching me.

My father grasped my wrist and hauled me away.

'Come on!' he said, pulling me outside.

He strode down the street and I had to run to keep up with him.

'Where does he live?'

'I don't know,' I said, holding my nose, which had started to bleed again. 'Waratah, I think.'

'Right, then.'

He hid the handle of the hammer up his sleeve, its head in his clenched hand. We walked in silence, except that every so often, he would mutter to himself, *'Poof,'* and then spit. (He wouldn't have cared that this word dates back to the nineteenth century, beginning as French slang for a prostitute.) When we finally came to Waratah I was exhausted. My father lifted me onto his back and asked what street the boy lived on. I told him again that I didn't know.

'All right,' he said. 'We'll look for him. Tell me when you see him.'

My father walked with me on his back for hours, peering into every garden and, if he could get close enough, every window of every house in every street in Waratah. After a long time it grew dark and I fell asleep. When I awoke we were at home again. I was lying on the couch and my father was holding my mother, who was crying.

'Stop greeting,' he said. 'Stop greeting, now. I couldn't find the bastard.'

'And what if you had?' she said, looking relieved and angry. 'What would we have done with you in jail, for assault, or worse?'

'All right.' He kissed her cheek. 'Will you not make us something to eat? We're starving.'

The next day was a Saturday. My father got dressed for work as usual, saying there was a chance for some overtime. While my mother was hanging out the washing, he rummaged in a kitchen cabinet where we kept all sorts of odds and ends. After he left, I went and looked there. Amongst all the old bills, receipts and blunt scissors, the phone book was open, with the page for 'Greer' to 'Gruenwald' ripped out.

No one at school ever called me a poof again.

TITS

Shortly before my twelfth birthday, a salesman came to our door selling volumes of the Longer Oxford English Dictionary. For a very reasonable rate, one of these thick books would be delivered to your home every month for two years. My mother, though she never bought anything from travelling salesmen, always invited them in, perhaps to make my father jealous. That day, he arrived home from the pub when the salesman was having a cup of tea. I was kneeling on the floor with the C open before me, so immersed in the dictionary that I didn't see my father until he nudged me with his foot.

'Whatever it is, we can't afford it,' he said. 'Give the book back to the man, son.'

My mother apologised to the salesman and my father saw him to the door. When he came back into the room, he whispered something to my mother and she smiled. A week later, for my birthday, I got A to Bea.

I would spend hours with the dictionary, learning all of the abbreviations – v.t. n pl colloq def MLG conj – and following words back in time to the places they were born. I discovered that many English words had come from other countries, like my father. I began to keep a notebook to write down the new words I invented – *umzob*, *caramot*, *grebulous* – and their imaginary meanings. By the time Gar to Hee was delivered, there were too many volumes for the bookshelf in my room and my mother moved them out into the garden shed, where they would be out of the way.

One afternoon, I went to look up 'carrion', a word I had come across while reading *The Count of Monte Cristo*. Caf to Dar was kept on a low shelf below my father's workbench. Sitting on the floor I pulled out the dictionary, but as I did so, a large loose square of chequered linoleum came away. Underneath the lino was a magazine, and on the front cover was a topless woman, cradling her gigantic breasts in her hands. The magazine was simply called *Tits* and was dated the month before. I began to look through it. After a few pages I grew bored of the breasts, all of them huge and thick-nippled. But I read on to examine all the different words for 'tits'. There were Bristols, titties, jugs, boobs, boobies, funbags, mammaries, pillows, baps. ('Tits' itself has an uncertain origin, but is similar to *titten* in German and *tieten* in Dutch.) Never before had I seen so many synonyms for one word. I had just opened my notebook to write them down when my father came in. I had my back to him, but he spotted the magazine and looked away, embarrassed, before realising it was only a pen I held in my hand. I got to my feet and he kicked the linoleum back over the magazine.

Then my mother was there. She was wearing a yellow dress and I noticed, for perhaps the first time, that she was flat-chested.

'Dinner's ready,' she said. 'What are you boys up to?'

My father didn't say anything.

'I was just showing Dad some new words I learned,' I said.

'You can show him at the table.'

After dinner, I wrote in my notebook, 'filicate n. a species of lie which a son tells for his father.'

PISS

During my last weeks at secondary school, my father had an accident. He was putting a new window in an office, standing three metres up on some scaffolding, when it began to rain heavily ('Absolutely pissing down,' he said when he told the story, ignoring my mother's frown.) As he hurried to finish the job, he slipped and fell onto the muddy ground below, breaking all of the ribs on his right side. For two months he lay in bed all day, smoking cigarettes and watching television. My mother took my room, because her tossing and turning kept him awake at night, and I slept on the sofa.

My father never complained of the pain, though for the first couple of weeks getting up to go to the toilet was agony for him. I had to support him as he urinated, hissing with the hurt. Three times a week his workmates would visit with slabs of beer. My mother didn't like alcohol. We didn't even have a corkscrew in the house. But seeing how the visits cheered my father, she said nothing. She didn't know that his friends would leave a dozen cans under the bed, which my father would drink, one after the other, when my mother was out. He said they were better for his ribs than the painkillers, but I knew he swallowed down the pills along with the beer. My father relied on me to air the room, buy him breath mints and dispose of the cans, and not to say anything to my mother. By now, I was very good at telling filicates.

One morning my father sent me on an errand to his friend who ran the local bottle-o. (This word formerly meant a person who sold and collected bottles. It comes from the cry, 'Bottle-oh!') After I paid him, he took me behind the counter and put a bottle of whisky in my bag.

'Remember, not a word to anyone,' he said. 'I would lose my job.'

I rode back home on my bike and gave the whisky to my father. He sent me out again to buy some sausage rolls for lunch and when I came back, the bottle was half-empty. He saw me frowning at it and said, 'Don't be such a pessimist. It's half-full. Now, what new words have you learned today?'

After drinking he always enjoyed a good sleep, and I hid the bottle away in my bedroom. It wasn't long before my father was sending me to the bottle-o every other day. I tried to stay away from the house so he couldn't ask me, but my mother wanted me nearby in case she needed me. A few weeks passed, and my mother went to visit her sister. I was studying in my room when I heard my father singing my name. I groaned and ignored him, until he began shouting. When I went in, he smiled and patted the seat beside the bed.

'Do you have any new words for me today?' he said.

'Yes,' I said, still standing in the doorway. 'Dipsomaniac.'

'That sounds like ... That sounds like a ... good one,' he said. 'What does it mean?'

'It's from the Greek, *dipsa*, meaning thirst, and the Latin, *mania*, indicating an extreme desire for something. Its short form is dipso.'

'I don't understand. What does it mean again?' my father asked.

'You should know it,' I said. 'It means "a drunk".'

My father nodded, and then as he realised what I had said, struggled to sit up.

'You don't know ...' he said. 'You don't know anything. How about you break a few of your ribs, see how you feel?'

He took a drink of whisky from a mug.

'Jesus Christ, you're a poor excuse for a son,' he mumbled. 'You and your books.'

I stared at him, and like a word that you look at for too long on the page, he began to lose any meaning for me.

'Well, here's a question for you,' he said at last. 'How many syllables are there in "Piss off"?'

In fact, I knew that 'piss' comes from the Middle English *pissen*, itself linked to the French *pissier*. But I said nothing. In response, he shouted at me, 'Go on, then. Piss off!'

I went to my books in the shed. An hour later, my mother came running from the kitchen.

'Come quick!'

My father was unconscious on the bedroom floor. Having drunk the rest of the whisky, he had been sick all over the sheets, and himself. Then he had fallen out of bed. The carpet around him was soaked with urine.

'Oh, Jimmy,' my mother wept.

I helped her strip and wash him. He groaned but didn't wake up. My mother changed the sheets and then, between the two of us, we got him back on the bed. Taking turns, we watched him through the night to make sure he didn't choke on his vomit.

When he awoke, he was penitent. Tears in his eyes, he swore to us that he wouldn't touch alcohol again. For the next two weeks I spent a lot of time with my father. Playing Scrabble kept his mind off the soreness, he said, and we had endless games together, though when we changed the rules to allow Doric, he won every time. In a while he was able to walk without much pain, and soon he was back at work.

On my way to the beach not long after, I saw my father sitting at a pub window, drinking. I rode home and searched my bookshelves until I found the notebook I was looking for. Opening it, I crossed out 'filicate' and went to tell my mother what I had seen.

SLUT

I was in my second year at university when my mother left my father. His drinking had gotten worse. If my mother begged, he would stop for a week or so, but it always started again. He was a good drunk, in that he was never violent and not usually unpleasant. The alcohol showed itself by a certain jerkiness as he talked. When he told all his old stories (including, inevitably, the one about the cock) his body seemed to respond, giving physical representations to parentheses, commas and question marks. By the end of an anecdote he was on his feet, clapping his right hand against his leg to mark full stops and stamping his feet for exclamation marks.

The only opportunity I had to study etymology was in Brisbane, so I wasn't able to come home much. During the holidays I rarely had enough money for travel, and even if I did, I made some excuse not to visit. At Christmas, however, there seemed to be no avoiding it. As it turned out, this would be the last time we were all together before the separation.

Christmas morning was quiet, my mother cooking an enormous lunch, my father watching television while I boxed up some books. I found the dictionary that my mother had spanked me with all those years ago. When I showed my father what he had written there, he was delighted.

'I mind that day well,' he said, and he began to hum 'Scotland the Brave'.

My mother heard him from the kitchen and laughed. After lunch, my father said, 'I'm going for a walk.'

'He'll come back drunk,' my mother said after he left. 'I never thought I'd have a drunk for a husband.'

I realised then how little I knew about my mother. I had often thought that the only way to truly understand a word was to know its past. But I knew almost nothing about my mother's.

'Who did you think you would marry?' I asked her.

For the next two hours we talked about the boys she had been in love with before my father, about her own mother and father, who I barely remembered, and about the good times when my father was courting her. Finally my father came home. He was, as my mother predicted, drunk. Having overheard her talking about my birth, he said, 'Yes, that was some day, some day. The best day of my life,' and my mother smiled at him.

'Almost as good was the day we conceived you,' he continued, winking at me.

'Jimmy! Don't!' my mother said, but my father had already started tapping his hand against his thigh. 'And it was the first time we did it. I remember you blushed, didn't you, May? And I said, "But you've seen my cock before," and then you giggled. Of course, we had to get married after that, when your father saw your belly. You said it was your first time, but that wasn't what I heard. You see, son, your mother was a bit of a slut in those days, and—'

She slapped him. It was the first time she had struck him since that afternoon in my grandparents' garden all those years before. The blood started leaking out of my father's nose, but this time my mother left the room and didn't come back and it was I who fetched a dishtowel for him. Without a word, my father took the towel, held it to his face and went out again, probably back to the pub. I found my mother in the shed, sobbing against the fourth volume of the dictionary, Caf to Dar, a place where I had always found comfort. The volume Ske to Tax noted that 'slut' was first recorded in English in 1402, originally meaning an untidy woman. It was only later that the word developed a sexual connotation. I tried to tell my mother this, but she wouldn't listen. So I put my arms around her and for a long time, neither of us said a word.

GOOK

After finishing uni, I got a job in Sydney working as an assistant lexicographer for the *Macquarie Dictionary*. I had just become engaged to Phuong, whom I had met in the first year of my studies. We drove down from Brisbane, stopping off at Coffs Harbour, where my mother now lived in a small unit, close to the ocean. When I introduced Phuong to her, she was delighted and immediately began to talk about grandchildren. Then she asked me when I had last seen Jimmy. For an instant, I didn't understand whom she meant. She had never spoken my father's Christian name to me before. He was always 'your father'. I told her we were going to drop by his place on our way south.

'I write to him every week,' she said. 'But he never replies.'

It was still Christmas at my father's house in Newcastle, as it had been for years. He had never taken down the decorations. There was a broken windowpane in one of the front windows; the flowerbeds were weedy, the grass long. I begged Phuong to wait in the car.

'You don't know him,' I said. 'I have to see what state he's in.'

I collected the mail and walked up to the house. I wondered if one of the envelopes contained the latest issue of *Tits* or perhaps one of my mother's letters, and then I wondered which would be more welcome to my father. I knocked on the door and he opened it.

My father was wearing a frayed dressing-gown my mother had bought him years before and he had a cigarette in his mouth. He had grown old and fat. He saw me looking at his belly and said through the smoke, 'Do I still have two feet, then? I haven't seen them in a while.'

He offered me his hand, which trembled a little, and I shook it.

'So where's this girl of yours?' he asked, stepping out onto the verandah. I waved at Phuong and she started to get out of the car.

'I thought Phuong was a funny name,' my father said, squinting. 'You never mentioned she was a gook.'

Without a word, I left my father there and marched down the path. Taking Phuong's hand, I led her back to the car.

'Son,' my father was calling, as he warily made his way down the steps. 'I'm sorry. I didn't mean it. I don't know why I ... She looks a lovely girl. Son!'

'What is it?' Phuong asked.

'We're going,' I said, opening the car door.

'Why?'

An 1893 dictionary of slang defines 'gook' as a low prostitute. It was adopted by American marines in the Philippine–American War to refer to all Filipinos (perhaps taken from 'Gugu', a mocking of Filipino speech) and extended throughout the twentieth century to embrace all South-East Asian countries, including Vietnam, where Phuong's parents had come from.

'I'll tell you on the way.'

'Son!' I heard him again, as we drove away. He jogged awkwardly after the car, then stopped and leaned over, holding his knees.

I didn't speak to him for five years.

FUCK

My mother called me from the hospital to tell me my father had suffered a stroke. He had telephoned her earlier that day, shouting unintelligibly into the phone. At first my mother thought that he was drunk, but something about his nonsense unsettled her. She immediately caught the train down. On arriving at the house she found him in the bedroom trying to pull his work overalls on. He had retired a year earlier. When he saw her, my father said thickly, 'What's for tea, May? I'm fucking starving.' His mouth was twisted and his right arm hung limp at his side.

My mother was sitting by his bed at the hospital when I got there. My father was asleep among the various wires and tubes that were keeping him alive. He was completely bald now and his skin had a yellow, coarse look, like the old newspapers you find under carpets. I kissed my mother, then leaned over to look more closely at my father. He opened his eyes, said quite clearly, 'Fuck!', and closed them again.

'The doctor said the stroke has affected his speech,' my mother said. 'He told me the name of it, but I can't remember. Dys-something. Or A-something-ia. It's the bit of the brain where you form words, where you choose them. The doctor said he can't censor himself. He's been swearing the whole time he's been in here. The doctor said, in the scans, there was evidence of older lessons in his brain. Lessons. Is that right?'

'Lesions?' I suggested.

'Yes, lesions. That maybe he had a small stroke years ago, and we never noticed, not with the drinking. And he said things … He couldn't stop himself from saying those bad things.' She began to cry.

'What's that fucking racket?' my father said, drowsily. 'I just want to sleep, for fuck's sake.'

We took him home three weeks later. He had lost almost all memory of the last ten years and his speech was confused. He would ask for a fork when he meant a knife, and call my mother a 'silly tart' when she brought him one. But then he would shake his head, saying, 'I'm sorry, hen. I can't help it. My fucking brain is fucked.'

When he was stronger, I introduced Phuong to him. My father took to her straight away and Phuong was fascinated by his swearing, especially the infinite uses he made of 'fuck', a word that can be traced back to the eighth century.

'Och, I don't give a fuck!' he would say when he disagreed, or 'Away to fuck!'

When she heard him, my mother would cry from wherever she was in the house, 'Oh, Jimmy! Can you please mind your language!' She had returned to look after him. I don't think he ever knew she had left.

After the stroke he never smoked or drank again. His speech became gradually more coherent but no less filthy. When I visited him he would shout, 'Come here, you daft bastard!' and embrace me. Then he would turn to my wife and, kissing her cheek, say, 'I don't know how he was smart enough to get someone like you, hen. He never had any common sense. As thick as pigshit, unstirred and undiluted. Except for his words. I'll give him that, the speccy bastard.'

In my father's curses was his blessing.

DAMN

My father came to live with us after my mother died. She was killed by a form of cancer that, up to the end, she was unable to pronounce. My father stayed at her side all the time she was dying. While she slept, he would pray to God, unconscious of his blasphemies.

'Our Father who art in fucking heaven,' he would plead, 'For fuck's sake, help my poor fucking wife.'

One evening, my father began to tell once more the story of the cock. 'Oh, Jimmy,' my mother said feebly. 'Not again.'

'Just listen,' he said. His recollection of that day was remarkable, although he had to stop half a dozen times when he couldn't find the word he wanted. Then my mother would help him.

'Greenhouse,' she would say softly. 'You were working on a greenhouse.'

As he neared the end of the story, I straightened up as – for the first time – he deviated from the well-rehearsed script of decades.

'Well,' he said, 'your mother went away to get a ... What is it? Fuck! Ah, a handkerchief because of my nose. And I thought ... And I thought to myself, "Jimmy, you've got to see this lassie again." So I took a whatdoyoucallit ... a rock. And I put a fucking crack in the lounge-room window!' He laughed. 'I cracked it, and I showed it to your mother so she would have me back again to fix it. So she would have me back ...'

My mother took his hand.

'You never told me that part,' she said. She looked happy and sad.

She died the next day.

My father was silent at the funeral, perhaps afraid of swearing in front of my mother's friends and relatives and making her ashamed of him yet again. He didn't say a word in the car or at the cemetery, where he stood holding my son's hand as my mother was laid to rest.

I drove my father back to the house to pack his things. When we arrived, he sat on the back deck as I shifted boxes into the van. It was dark by the time I finished and he was still sitting there. I went out and sat beside him.

'Damn,' he said.

'What is it?'

'That's the only time your mother ever fucking swore at me,' my father said quietly. 'Just the once. She said, "Damn you, Jimmy."'

I didn't tell my father that 'damn' comes from the Middle English, *dampen*, itself derived from the Latin, *damnare*, to condemn, to inflict loss. He already knew exactly what it meant.

For a moment I could think of no word to comfort him. Then I cried out, 'When!' and without a second's pause my father farted, loudly, enormously.

And throwing back his head he roared his laughter at the darkness.

SEVENTEEN RULES FOR WRITING A SHORT STORY

1. 'Every character should want something, even if it is only a glass of water.'—Kurt Vonnegut

Andrew's throat was dry. He crossed into the shade and looked about the wide street for a shop. The heat was making the buildings, trees and road shimmer, as if the world was in doubt of its own existence. It suddenly came upon him that he had no idea where he was. Turning into a narrow alleyway he eventually emerged onto a main road, already hectic with buses and cars. At last, he found a small café and, seating himself, poured some water from a bottle into a glass and drank it.

'Ah, that's better,' he said.

2. 'Use short sentences and short first paragraphs.'— Ernest Hemingway

Andrew was thirsty. He crossed the street. It was hot. He was lost. The traffic was busy. He went to a café. He drank some water. It was nice.

3. 'My own experience is that once a story has been written, one has to cross out the beginning.'—Anton Chekhov

~~Andrew was thirsty. He crossed the street. It was hot. He was lost. The traffic was busy. He went to a café. He drank some water. It was nice.~~

After leaving the café, Andrew managed to find his way home, staying in the shade as much as he could. Mona was waiting for him at the front door, sweating in a too-tight red dress that gave her skin a sheen like the cover of a fashion magazine.

4. 'I like it when there is some feeling of threat or sense of menace in short stories. I think a little menace is fine to have in a story.'—Raymond Carver

'Your brother is here,' Mona shivered.

'What?' Andrew breathed. 'John's out of prison?'

A single bead of sweat trickled down the side of his face.

'I thought he wasn't up for parole for another ten years.'

Six heavy footsteps, then the lounge-room door creaked open, and Andrew's brother loomed.

5. 'I think it's a good idea to write a little – about two lines, not more, or three lines – about any person you wish.'—V.S. Pritchett

John was a large man with sullen eyes and red hair. His face was pitted with blackheads, like the dots that had made up his photograph in the newspaper accounts of the trial.

6. 'Short stories can be rather stark and bare unless you put in the right details. Details make stories human, and

*the more human a story can be, the better.'—Katherine
Mansfield*

Andrew remembered when they were boys, how his mother
would draw a map of the bruises on his legs before he went
to play with John, and how she would beat John if she found
any new bruises at the end of the day. Sometimes, when he was
angry with his brother, Andrew deliberately scraped his shin so
that John would be punished.

'Hello, Andy,' John said. 'You've gotten fat.'

John always opened their conversations with an insult as a
way of testing Andrew's mood, in the same way he would spit on
a griddle to see if it was hot. There was a new tattoo on his neck,
Andrew noticed, of a spider's web, the blue strands of webbing
inked in such a way that they included the thick veins, one leg
of the spider just visible above the neckline of John's cotton
T-shirt.

John walked quickly forward and Andrew flinched, but his
brother only wanted to

7. *'A short story is a photograph.'—Lorrie Moore*

8. *'Find the key emotion; this may be all you need know to find your short story.'*—F. Scott Fitzgerald

John smiled at him, but wouldn't relax his grip. Andrew was terrified. He had no idea what to do.

9. *'When in doubt, have two guys come through the door with guns.'*—Raymond Chandler

'Police! Get down!'
'Come and get me!' John screamed!

10. *'Cut out all exclamation points. An exclamation point is like laughing at your own joke.'*—John Dos Passos.

'Police. Get down.'
'Come and get me,' John screamed.

11. *'To me, the greatest pleasure of writing is not what it's about, but the inner music the words make.'*
—Truman Capote

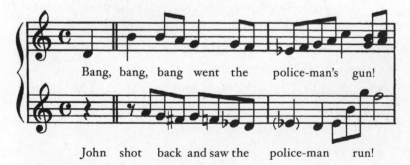

Bang, bang, bang went the police-man's gun!

John shot back and saw the police-man run!

12. 'No matter how sweet and innocent your leading characters, make awful things happen to them – in
order that the reader may see what they are made of.'—
Kingsley Amis

The first bullet tore off Mona's left ear, the next collapsed her
lung, and the last lodged near her heart. Andrew screamed as
she fell and John punched him in the face, knocking out three
of his teeth.

13. 'A story to me means a plot where there is some
surprise.'—Isaac Bashevis Singer

John cradled Mona in his arms.
  'Don't die,' he whispered. 'I love you.'
  'You never knew ...' Mona said. 'I had your baby. Years ago. I
gave him up for adoption. You see, Andrew would never ...'
  'I'm gay,' Andrew sobbed.

14. 'The more a story cooks, the better.'—Doris Lessing

'I'm dying, Andrew,' Mona gasped. 'You'll have to make dinner.
Remember to cook the bacon in a large pan. Then you have to
sauté the beef for exactly eight minutes. Don't crowd it! You
could put in a little seasoning. Maybe some salt. Finally, add
the bacon and garlic to the meat, and some stock. Then bring it
to a boil. Let it simmer for half an hour. Drain, and serve with
parsley ... For God's sake, serve with ...'

15. 'If a writer knows enough about what he is writing
about, he may omit things that he knows.'
—William Faulkner

'Why did you come here?' Andrew cried.

'You know why,' John said.

'But it was so long ago,' Andrew said.

'I haven't forgotten anything,' John replied.

> 16. *'What would there be in a story of happiness? Only what prepares it, only what destroys it can be told.'*
> —*André Gide*

Mona perished. John went back to prison, for life this time. Andrew died of a broken heart.

> 17. *'Finish a story you start.'*—*Colm Tóibín*

The End.

A SPEEDING BULLET

This is my secret origin.

I was born and grew up in a neat yellow house in Newcastle. In memory, it has always a single white oval cloud floating above it, like an empty speech bubble. I remember especially the lantana behind the house where one summer I cut a secret base. On our street there were only three houses and I was the only child. The road was long and narrow and crooked off at one end like a life of virtue corrupted.

*

On my ninth birthday, as my mother walked home from the shops, she came across hundreds of American comic books left by the roadside, stacked haphazardly beside an ancient rocking chair and a broken toy truck. She had heard that the old man, Mr Kirby, who lived nearby had recently died, and his relatives were clearing out his house. Mr Kirby had spoken to me a few times. He liked to brush my bare arm with his long fingers as he asked me about school. The touch of those fingers was as fleeting and light as a fly's, and as with flies you somehow knew the last thing they had touched was something unclean.

One day my father went to see Mr Kirby and he never came near me again.

*

My mother, knowing how much I loved to read *The Phantom* in the newspaper, piled some comics in the three-wheeled toy truck, making several trips to drag them all home. She then called me from my den in the lantana (which that day became my Fortress of Solitude), where I was playing with our dog, Buster (who from that day, to his lasting confusion, became Krypto, after Superman's dog). Though it wasn't hot, my mother was breathless and flushed, for she was very fat. She left the truck by the new bike that lay on the neatly mown grass. This was my birthday present. I hated bikes, but my father thought it was time I learned how to ride one. He had promised to teach me, but he was out drinking with his friends.

*

I can still recall the cover of the comic on top of the pile, *The Justice Society of America*. 'A Titanic Struggle Between Good and Evil,' the blocky red lettering proclaimed. 'And a Hero shall FALL!!' I spent the rest of the afternoon slowly reading through dozens of comic books: Marvel, DC, Fawcett, EC, Timely.

I remember the costumes and battles, the splash pages and panels, word and thought balloons, advertisements for sea monkeys and Charles Atlas weightlifting manuals ('I Can Make YOU a New Man, Too, in Only 15 Minutes a Day'). The peculiar

American spelling had such an effect on me that to this day, even after ten years as a journalist, I still spell 'colour' without a u.

*

When my father returned from the pub he wanted me to go on the bike, but I said that it was too late and went on reading about the Elongated Man. That night I couldn't sleep for thinking of the Sub-Mariner, the Challengers of the Unknown, Doctor Strange, Mr Mxyzptlk, Bizarro. I felt as if I had put two fingers down the throat of my imagination.

My favourite hero was Captain Marvel. His alter-ego was a nine-year-old boy like me, called Billy Batson. When he said his secret magic word – 'Shazam!' – he was transformed into the heroic Captain, a superhero who was all grown up.

'Shazam!' I whispered to myself in bed that night. When at last I fell asleep, I dreamed four-color dreams.

*

My father, Michael Shields, was born in England in 1939, the same year that Batman first appeared. At the age of eighteen he joined the army and eventually rose to the rank of sergeant. (When I showed him the Marvel comic *Sgt Fury and His Howling Commandos*, he laughed and said it wasn't like that at all. I didn't believe him.) After an honourable discharge he came to Australia in the sixties, met my mother and became a policeman. He was very tall and strong, and handsome in his uniform. But when he was thinking of something hurtful to say to my mother his lips would work up and down and an ugly look would come upon his face. I had seen this look upon my own face once in the mirror, when I was chewing a scab. Although my father rarely raised his voice, he spoke to my mother with jagged lines around his words, as in comics when people screamed.

He hated foreigners, especially Asians. Often at dinner he would tell of stopping a 'Chinky' and fining them for no reason. He would put his front teeth out over his lower lip and singsong, 'Oh, me so solly officah!' I would laugh, though my mother scowled at us and begged him not to talk that way. But I had read about Captain America fighting Japanese spies in World War II and I knew they sounded exactly like that.

*

My mother wore huge flowery dresses and had long brown hair and a round face with sad brown eyes. Old photographs showed a different woman, thin and smiling, so that I began to think all her fat was a disguise, like Superman's glasses. She was very gentle, but she always had an exhausted and agonised air, as if she had just been taken down from a cross.

*

The day after my birthday, I was reading an issue of *Detective Comics* when my father came home. He was wearing his uniform and his gun. In my lap, Commissioner Gordon was asking Batman to help capture the Mad Hatter.

'Will you be commissioner one day, Dad?' I asked.

'Maybe. One day,' he said, sitting down.

'You look a bit like one of the policemen helping Batman. Commissioner Gordon.'

'Do I? And who does your mother look like?'

'Well, no one in this issue,' I said. 'But I have a *Wonder Woman* in my room. Her hair is like Wonder Woman's.' And my mother smiled at me from the kitchen, where she was peeling potatoes.

My father laughed and picked up an issue of *The Uncanny X-Men* from the floor. 'Who is this fellow?' he said. On the cover, Cyclops was punching an enormous obese man.

'That's The Blob. He's an evil Mutant. He fights against the X-Men.'

'Do you hear that?' he called to my mother. 'The Blob! That's who you look like.'

My mother turned back to the potatoes, muttering something about Jesus.

'"Jesus", she says. Have you ever read the Bible, son?' my father said. 'It's full of superheroes, like her man Jesus.'

He rolled up the comic and poked me in the stomach with it.

'Anyway, I'd better see you riding that bike by the weekend. I paid good money for it, and I didn't steal it from a rubbish tip either.'

He went to take off his uniform.

*

The day after I finally succeeded in cycling up and down the street, I pretended to be The Atom. I squeezed into my wardrobe to read an issue of *The Doom Patrol* and then I crawled down the hall and into my parents' bedroom. I could just fit under the bed. It was very dusty and I found a pile of magazines which at first I took to be more comics. The women in the photographs had the same ridiculous proportions as comic-book heroines. But they had no uniforms, no clothes in fact, and their legs, not their arms, were spread for flight. I stayed under there for a while, looking at the pictures, until I heard my father's voice from the hall. Then I kept very still.

They were fighting again. There was my name. Comics. The bike. Both their voices were jagged now. A short silence and then a sound. It wasn't a *Ka-Pow!* or a *Kerrack!* It was a hollow, wet smack. My father hit my mother three or four times. I couldn't tell precisely how many because I had my hands over my ears. But I must have had super-hearing because I could still make out all the words he called her, and I could hear my mother bawling my father's name, as if it had some magic to it, like *Shazam!*

'You disgust me, you fat blob,' my father said, before he slammed the front door. My mother stood in the hall for a long time.

*

Later, when I came in from the garden, I saw her. She was wearing so much make-up she looked a little like The Joker. She smiled at me and asked me about the stories I had read that afternoon.

'Did the heroes win?'

I shook my head. My father was reading the paper. He looked up at me and winked.

'Found any Australian supermen yet?' he asked. I shook my head again. I was silent until I went to bed.

I thought about the leader of the Inhumans, a melancholy man called Black Bolt. He didn't dare speak because a single syllable from his lips had the power to destroy a city. For the rest of the week, I was Black Bolt. My parents fought every night and never noticed that I nodded and shook my head instead of speaking. Even when I closed my eyes, I could see them fighting. I wondered if Superman could see through his eyelids with his X-Ray vision.

*

My mother called me in from the Fortress of Solitude. She and my father were in the living room. My mother had been crying again and her face was swollen. It was a humid day and she was sweating even more than usual, her hair standing up as if she had been given a shock by Electro. She wore a dirty red dress that had been discolored blue after being washed with my father's uniform, and there was a triangular sweat stain on her chest like a soiled Superman symbol. Slumped in the armchair, she looked badly drawn.

My father was ready for his night shift. He was clean-shaven and his uniform was neat and ironed. He posed in the doorway as if it were a panel from a comic book and he the hero, with his polished belt and cap and gun.

'Your mother's just told me she wants to leave,' he said. 'She says she isn't happy here with you and me.'

'That's not—' my mother began.

'Shut up!' my father said. 'She wants to take you away, son. Away from your home. Away from your dad. Do you want to go with her?'

I looked at my father, standing in the light, his arms folded, then at my mother, biting her nails and staring, red-eyed, at me. I felt all-powerful, as Black Bolt must have felt, because I could destroy everything with one word.

'No,' I said. My father grinned at me and ruffled my hair. I was his Boy Wonder.

'Do you want to walk me to the station?' he asked. I didn't look at my mother, but I could hear her crying. I imagined two wet word balloons over her head. 'SOB! SOB!'

I went out into the sunlight with my father. Arms outstretched, I swooped around him until he tired of me and sent me home before we were a hundred yards from the house.

*

I found my mother when I returned from school that Friday. She had taken my father's old revolver from a shoebox in the cupboard and shot herself through the heart.

Comics had taught me that death was impermanent. Heroes and villains could die, but they always came back to life a few issues later, through sorcery, or time-travel, or the Lazarus Pit. Even my mother's favourite superhero, Jesus Christ, had risen from the dead.

But when I saw the red of her blood I knew my mother was gone forever. No comic-book panel ever had such a color.

*

I believed there was no mystery about my mother, but I was wrong. Seven years after she died, the same year I would leave my father's house for good, I came across her birth certificate in the back of a drawer. My father and everyone who knew my mother had called her Martha, but the paper showed she was christened Diana. I never found out why she had changed her name. I suppose all parents have secret identities they hide from their children.

*

My father died ten years after my mother. In the fifties, while still in the army, he had been stationed in the Pacific, near the atomic bomb tests. The radiation didn't grant him spider-sense, or turn him invisible. Instead it gave him pancreatic cancer and he died in agony, crying for his wife.

*

I stopped reading comic books when I started going out with girls. If they commented on a stray *Ghost Rider* on my bedroom floor, I would amuse them with speculations about the sex life of Mr Fantastic, who could stretch any body part, or the Multiple Maid, who could enjoy a *ménage à trois* with herself.

Eventually I married, perhaps because my wife had an alliterative name. I told her my parents had died in a plane crash, like Peter Parker's. But shortly after our honeymoon she found out about my mother's suicide. Before I returned from the newspaper that evening, she threw all my comics away.

We have a son who loves to read. He reads anything: instructions for the television, electricity bills, the ingredients of toothpaste. He reads as if he were being examined in the morning on how to live, how to exist. I sometimes wonder if he would be happier as an orphan – Robin was always laughing, after all. Last week he brought home a comic book, the latest issue of *Captain Marvel*. I borrowed it from him and read it on the train to work. Dr Sivana was still plotting the destruction of Keystone City, and Billy Batson hadn't changed at all. He was still nine years old. And so, I realised, was I.

Every night now, I say the magic word very quietly, so my wife won't hear. It helps me to sleep. And perhaps I believe that if I say it often enough the magic bolt of lightning will strike, and I will stand a foot taller, caped and smiling, then wink at my astonished wife and fly far away from here.

'Shazam,' I whisper. 'Shazam. Shazam. Shazam!'

THE CHINESE LESSON

In the park, the old women were walking backwards. Watt waited beneath the enormous statue of a rifle grasped in a clenched stone fist. It was as if China itself were taking aim at God, he thought. He pushed his round glasses back onto his nose, to stop the world from slipping from his eyes. As he waited he took a chipped blue disc from his pocket and twisted it in his hand. Lingering in front of the large painted map of the park bolted to the base of the statue, he studied the Chinese characters and their English translations. A small, primary-coloured pagoda on a nearby hill was, he discovered, the Chinese–Vietnam People's Blood-Soaked Friendship Pavilion, while the dirty lake behind him was something to do with fragrant happiness. At least he could understand the English. Chinese characters were little mazes, like those he had liked to solve in activity books as a boy.

Unable to find a way out of the character for 'lake', Watt looked up and saw Xia Meng walking through the park gates, holding books in her hands as a waiter might carry an overfull tray. She was wearing a white blouse with nonsensical English printed all over it. Xia Meng was a Chinese teacher and translator, and it was she who had written the English on the sign. Watt returned the disc to his pocket and went towards her. It was an overcast day, not cold, yet still he walked with hunched shoulders, staring at the ground.

They met at a mossy bench by the lake, greeting each other so formally they might have been speakers A and B in an English textbook dialogue. Then they sat down on the bench with their notepads on their laps, looking out over the water. It was dark and showed no reflections, as if it had drowned the sky in its murk.

'Now,' Xia Meng said. She had long dark hair and sleep in the corners of her eyes from staying up late to study. 'We are continuing "The Market", aren't we today?'

'No,' Watt said. 'Today I want to do "Travel".'

'Why, Lawrie?' she asked. Although they had been sleeping together for two and a half years, they still could not pronounce each other's name properly. While he had given up on hers, she would still practise his every night as she translated press releases, mouthing, "Red lorry, yellow lorry" again and again. But the r's always straightened themselves into l's, and the l's stooped over to become r's.

Watt's eyes smarted from the factory smoke. It seemed to give the air a grain, almost as if it were paper. He remembered a game they used to play. Xia Meng would pull the skin around his eyes to slit them, pretending he was Chinese, and he would hold her eyelids between his finger and thumb, and pretend she was European. Watt took off his glasses and cleaned them on his shirt.

'We studied "Travel" last month,' she said. 'You know, your vocabulary of food is very limited. We ought to really practise that, so you can start going to the market, instead of me all the time.'

'No. "Travel",' he insisted.

Xia Meng's left foot trembled, making a little grave for itself in the dirt.

'I can never understand you,' she said. 'All last week till now, it is I want to study marketing and now it is "Travel". I don't understand you at all. Sometimes I wish I could read a biography of you.'

'You would have to be the one to write it,' he said.

'And I would write only bad things,' she said, frowning.

'I want to do "Travel",' he whispered, 'for the honeymoon.'

She smiled, looking past him to watch a little boy as he picked up a pebble, threw it in the water, and then stepped back at the splash as if he expected the lake to overflow. Watt glanced at his watch.

'What time is it?' she asked him.

'In English? Ten past two.'

'No, in Chinese.'

'In Chinese?'

He watched the boy's mother pick him up, take down his trousers and hold him above the bin so he could defecate into it. 'About five hundred years ago, I think.'

'You are very humorous,' she said. 'Let's start the lesson now. "Travel." Very well. "I am a teacher from Australia." Say it in Chinese.'

Watt tried the words and Xia Meng corrected him. His Chinese was appalling. Shopkeepers and bus conductors always assumed he was speaking English, even when he was saying the most simple Mandarin phrases.

'Your pronunciation is still not very good,' she said. She paused over the characters in the book before them, then said suddenly, 'Tell me again. What is Australia like?'

'Koalas,' Watt said. 'Kangaroos. Hats with corks.'

'It is a very new country, isn't it?' she asked.

'Yes. My ancestors were the kind of people your ancestors built the Great Wall to keep out.'

She laughed. Watt looked across the lake at the pagoda on the hill, where he had first been alone with Xia Meng. From there you could see into the zoo, which contained a miserable lion and a reptile enclosure. On a small chair amid the snakes, terrified children were placed to have their pictures taken. Near the pagoda was the playground, where old men hung on the monkey bars or seesawed together for morning exercise. Watt could see a very young soldier sitting on a swing. He didn't seem to take his uniform seriously, as if he were an extra in a war movie. His prop rifle leaned against the ice-cream stand.

Watt hated Chinese parks, how they domesticated the landscape, plucked the sting from the drifting wasps, turning their meandering hum into that of a refrigerator. The few gulls in the sky were like a child's mobile, and the only trees he could see were the poorly painted ones on the walls of the public toilets. He looked at his watch again, then at Xia Meng as she wrote the Chinese characters for 'airplane' and 'ticket'. Her handwriting was not as graceful as he was used to seeing from his students. The left-handedness had been beaten out of her in primary school. When she had finished, he took the pen and copied the characters into his notebook. Occasionally she corrected his strokes.

'Very good,' she said at last. 'It will be funny when my name is Watt because it sounds like "what". Did you know?'

'Yes, I knew,' Watt said. 'How would I say, "A one-way ticket to Beijing? Hard sleeper."'

She told him how to ask for the train ticket.

'Can I see you write it?' Again he watched her and copied her strokes, much more carefully this time.

'How is that?' he asked.

'Excellent!' Xia Meng said. 'You are a good student!'

The smile left her face as she saw a pregnant woman walk past. The woman had no belly yet, but still she wore large, loose green dungarees embroidered with white rabbits. Watt and Xia Meng both sat watching the water for some time, like bored sightseers. Then she began to cry quietly, her hands resting in her lap. After a moment, she reached over to his jacket, which lay on the bench between them, looking for a tissue. Watt took the jacket away from her and, searching the pockets himself, brought out a clean white handkerchief.

'When can I wear clothes like that?' Xia Meng said, wiping her face. 'I am more pregnant than her!'

'Soon,' he said. 'You know you're allowed more than one child because you're with a foreigner. You can wear clothes like that all the time. I'll keep you as pregnant as a Catholic, if that's what you want.'

'What's a Catholic?' she asked him, sniffing.

'Just an animal,' he said. 'It likes to have sex, and then feels bad afterwards.'

Upset as she was, Xia Meng made careful note of this new word and its definition in her notebook. It was full of things Watt had made up as a joke. He had often meant to tell her the real meanings, but never had.

'What do you want me to do?' he asked her.

'You know,' she said. 'We must tell my mother, and then we must get married. Not to get married after all this, it is impossible.'

Watt thought of Xia Meng's mother, a bitter old woman whose face was not so much wrinkled as creased, like the lines on the palm of a hand.

'If your mother is happy that you're having a bastard with a foreigner, then I'm a ...' he laughed. 'I'm a bloody Chinaman.'

'Do not swear, Lawrie, please,' she said.

'Don't cry,' he said. 'We'll tell her tonight, if you want.'

'Do you mean it?'

'Of course.'

'Oh, Lawrie! Red lorry, yellow lorry!' she grasped his hand under the wooden table. 'I love you. We will be so happy!'

A bald man carrying a newspaper hawked and spat a little China of bacteria at their feet. Watt looked at him in disgust. Xia Meng hadn't noticed.

'You should go back to the flat and change,' he said. 'I'll go buy a new shirt. We should both look our best tonight.'

'Yes, wonderful!' she said.

They walked together to the park gates, then past shops with names that had long since ceased to amuse him: 'Classy Lady', 'Soft Lass', 'Smelling Beautiful Food'. Watt gave Xia Meng a hundred yuan for the lesson, which she would pass on to the agency she worked for. As she took the money, she stroked his hand. He watched her get on a bus. She waved to him from the window as it drove away. Watt couldn't see her face because he found himself trying to make out the words on her blouse.

As the bus turned the corner, he tore a page from his notebook and then threw the book in the bin. He went towards the crowded square in front of the train station. Passing the rows of hairdressers that were really brothels, he saw the prostitutes standing behind empty chairs, playing with scissors and pretending to cut each other's hair. In the square there were hundreds of Chinese sitting or standing beside enormous striped plastic bags. Most of the men were smoking, and almost all of them wore brown of one shade or another. They were like a nation in camouflage. Watt found the left-luggage office and took the blue disc from his pocket to give to the attendant, who wore a surgical mask. He looked in the shelves behind him, then handed Watt a black suitcase. Watt hefted it to the ticket office and, after queuing for a long time, handed over the note that he had copied from Xia Meng and paid for his ticket to Beijing.

'Thank you,' he said in English, and the lovely young clerk smiled shyly at him.

As he waited on the platform, Watt took his glasses from his irritated eyes. But no matter how much he polished the lenses, the world would become no cleaner.

A STORY IN WRITING

This story is set in Muloobinba, a fictional analogue of Newcastle, New South Wales. Located two hours north of Sydney, it has a population of just over 400,000. The decaying buildings of this industrial city bloom with graffiti and the horizon is cluttered with coal ships. Our story is concerned with three upper-middle-class characters who live in Rooks Hill, Muloobinba's most affluent suburb.

The story proper begins on 26 March 2009 at 2.34 p.m., with a tennis ball being served at a broken-down court in the poorer suburb of Brayfield, and concludes on 13 January 2010 with a *

FREE VERSE

the two men
played tennis
without
a

94

net

i liked your last story

penn backhanded.

not a bad effort.

and how is the novel?

frank returned.

out! penn cried. next year, i hope.

are you coming tonight?

to the reading?

penn asked.

callie asked me to ask.

of course i'm coming.

what's the score?

me forty

and you

love.

PROTAGONIST

Frank Wright is a lean, tall man with thinning black hair. After a lifetime of reading, he appears to have absorbed several letters of the alphabet. There is a bad-tempered v between the o's of his blue eyes, and a dimple resembling an inverted e on his prominent chin. He has a strange habit of carefully collecting and storing his toenail clippings as if they were the relics of a medieval saint.

Frank is an English teacher in a secondary school, but regards his true vocation as being a writer. He has had several stories published in literary journals and one collection, which *Australian Book Review* said was 'Not entirely a failure'. He has been married for nine years to Esther, but regards their relationship as an irrelevant subplot in his life story. Already, he has made a secret will, leaving her only the second-best bed.

BIBLICAL

1. And Francis, son of Alan, was much vexed by this defeat at the hands of his foe, Penn, son of Jacob, on the field of tennis.
2. And he returned, filled with wrath, to his dwelling, in the street of Maud, in the land of Muloobinba.
3. And the anger of Francis was hot against Penn, the Philistine scribe, and the success of the man did oppress him.
4. In the bitterness of his soul he wanted the relief of knowing a woman.
5. Therefore he called upon his wife, Esther, Esther, but answer she did not.
6. And then he bethought him of the harlot named Callie, daughter of Jason, who was the woman of Penn, son of Jacob.
7. And it came to pass that he did evil in the sight of the LORD, as he took himself in hand and cried out, Callie.
8. And he did spill his seed upon the ground.
9. Then behold, he came up out of the bedroom and into the bathroom, to purify himself before the LORD.

HOMERIC SIMILE

Like a thunderous waterfall when it plummets over the edge of the earth, rainbowing the sky with its spray while endlessly wearying away the rocks, so Frank pissed in the toilet bowl.

ANAGRAMS

Farnk dah a whores dan tog dreesds. Ti saw stomal ixs o'klocc, nad het pyoter degrain aws ta evens. Eh cadell tou a gybedoo ot shi fiew dan tefl. Sa eh ardeen het kophsobo ti tetrads ot nair. Eh delf thiw gustisd morf het poniardsr sa fi yeth reew splitet.

Deisin, het boskopho aws wordedc. Eh was Pnne lungingo anti-
sag Pyreto nad eh tewn pu ot klat ot mih.

DEUTERAGONIST

Michael Penn is Frank's oldest friend. They have known each
other for over twenty years. Penn resembles Frank in many
ways, though he is undoubtedly uglier and clumsier, like a
bad translation of a book from a foreign language. Penn was
once a performance poet but is now a novelist. His first novel,
Australasia, wasn't shortlisted for the Vogel and received no
acclaim when it was eventually brought out by a vanity press.
Nevertheless, its publication secured him a job as a creative
writing tutor at the local university. He is currently at work on
his second novel.

For the past few years, Penn has been reading James Joyce's
Ulysses. He carries the book with him everywhere. Upon finishing
a page he rips it out and leaves it wherever he happens to be. Penn
says that he hopes someone will find and read one of the pages
and be transfigured by the prose. So far, this has not happened.

ANNOTATION

'Did you get much done today?' Frank asked, sipping his wine.[1]
   'Yes,' Penn said, rubbing his back against Biography.[2] 'About
a thousand words, after our tennis game.[3] By the way, I read that
anonymous review of your book in *Easterly*. He had no right to
say what he did. No right.'

---

1   Chateau D'Orsay, 2008.

2   Penn suffers from eczema between his shoulderblades.

3   This is a lie. He wrote nothing.

'It might have been a woman,' Frank said, glancing over Penn's shoulder to see if he could spot a copy of his book.[4]

'Of course, of course,' Penn said.

Frank looked around for Callie, but all he could see was her picture on the cover of her poetry collection,[5] displayed against one wall.

'Where's Callie?' he asked. 'Isn't the reading supposed to start now?'

'She's outside, having a smoke. Just nerves. Where's Esther?'[6]

'At home. Feeling a bit under the weather, so she couldn't come.'[7]

'That's a shame,' Penn said.[8] 'How is married life?'

'Like working on a story every day and knowing it will never be good enough to publish,'[9] Frank said. 'And how is living in sin with Callie?'

'Quite sinful enough,' Penn smiled. 'Oh, wait a minute. There she is.'

Frank watched Callie appear from a door in the back of the bookshop. There was scattered applause as she made her way through the crowd, brushing past Frank and Penn, to the microphone. Frank picked up a biography of John Howard[10] and held on to it throughout Callie's reading.

---

4   There were none. His collection had sold poorly and hadn't been reprinted.

5   *Sappho in Sydney* by Callie Reid, Ten Islands Press, 2009.

6   **Unseen Character.** Despite being referred to several times, Frank's wife never actually appears in the story.

7   Frank didn't tell Esther about the poetry launch. She thinks he is at the library.

8   He enjoyed looking at Esther's large breasts.

9   Frank is quoting from his own short story, 'The Writer', third runner-up in Muloobinba City Council's 2005 short-story competition.

10   To hide a sudden erection.

Tritagonist

Callie Reid has long blonde hair, an eternal half-smile and fine, pale skin. She is very beautiful, though her beauty seems somehow forced and artificial, as if she is frozen in her own author's photograph. She has been seeing Michael Penn for six months. Callie is a poet, and her author bio vaguely mentions her winning a number of competitions, while not revealing that these were all held in her secondary school. At present, she is studying for a Masters of Creative Writing at Muloobinba University. Michael is her tutor.

Ellipsis

... began to read ... 'I love my lover like no other,' she finished ... said Penn and Frank nod ... the crowd ... applauded while ... and she ... at first ... champagne ... smiled ... 'Flatterer!' she cried and playfully ... 'Why don't we' ... 'Your place, Michael' ... three of them left for ... Frank said, 'I loved your use of ellip ...

Archaic

'Zounds!' Penn did cry, his visage sanguine with the grape. 'Truly, this was an eve anacreontic!'

He belched at the tenebrous welkin.

'Another goblet, Francis? Repugn me not!'

'I am glutted! I am glutted!'

'How now, my cove!' Mistress Callie did snort. 'Thou must sup!'

'I mote,' Francis said, extending his cup.

The triumvirate was ensconced in the gardens of Penn's estate, Callie lying betwixt Penn and Francis, a dozen resplendent

99

terebinths melodious in the gloaming. Of a sudden, Penn farted.

'By Christ, that reeks of cag-mag!' Francis yowled.

'In truth, those wittles from Indya have fair wrenched mine belly,' Penn cried. 'I cannot thole it. To the pissoir I go!'

Exit Penn.

'This is opportune,' Francis did say, taking Mistress Callie in his arms.

'Mind thy pickers and stealers, my lord! There'll be no rantipoling here!' she retorted, pushing him away. 'I bethink me thou art far from uxorious.'

'Aye, not uxorious, merely precipitous,' he exclaimed. 'I would not vitiate thy good lord's friendship, but squalls and windstorms are revening my heart. Gramercy! I do love thee.'

'Be not lachrymose, for the love of God,' she did say. 'I cannot bear a lugubrious man. Thou art befuddled with wine.'

'Make not thy moues at me,' he begged. 'I say again, I do love thee. Wilt thou give me quietus or salvation, thou must choose! Quickly now! He cometh!'

'Thou hast blunted me!' she did say. 'We shall meet this Sabbath noonday, at the sign of the Simians Three.'

'I gloat on joyous pinions,' he laughed, kissing of her hand.

Enter Penn.

'What tenesmus was that!' Penn did roar, appearing on the colonnade. 'Methought I was shitting a basilisk!'

CHARACTONYMS

Frank Wright: Francis de Sales is the patron saint of writers and Wright is a heterograph of 'write'.

Callie Reid: Calliope was the muse of epic poetry in Greek mythology. Reid is, of course, a homophone of 'read'.

Michael Penn: Penn is simply 'pen' with an extra n.

Hyperbole

Frank and Callie sat together in the café, the only two people in the world.

'It seems like eons since I last saw you,' he asseverated.

'Doesn't it? I absolutely adore this place,' she gushed. 'Isn't it too wonderful?'

'Ah, yes. The Three Monkeys. It's the best café in the world,' Frank agreed wholeheartedly.

Callie laughed uproariously.

'You're the most amusing man I've ever known,' she ejaculated.

'You are a goddess, you know,' he murmured, trying to take her hand. 'What extraordinary fingers you have.'

'Horrible, pudgy things,' she grimaced, freeing herself. 'Shall we order?'

He nodded emphatically.

'I could eat a horse,' Frank beamed.

They asked for the most astronomically expensive items on the menu and ate in complete and utter silence.

'How is Esther?' Callie demanded after a million years.

'One's wife should not be one's life,' he moaned.

'But she is the finest woman ...'

'I would leave her in a nanosecond,' Frank declaimed.

'And Michael is the dearest man, you know,' Callie said with infinite sadness.

'A new Hemingway,' he soothed. 'I despise him. I'll die a lingering death without you.'

'I live in a hovel,' she cried. 'But would you care to feast your eyes upon it?'

'There is nothing in the world I would like more.'

As they walked through the streets, deserted as if for Judgment Day, Callie pointed upwards.

'Isn't that the most beautiful thing you've ever seen?' she said, weeping.

HAIKU

lights on an airplane
a red blue constellation
adrift in the sky

CALLIGRAM

                              he said.
                         breathless
                     making me
                that is
             it's you
          she said.
       broken
     lift is
   and the
  sixth floor
 on the
i live

DIGRESSION

The first elevator, according to the Roman architect Vitruvius, was designed by Archimedes circa 236 BC. Elevators appeared throughout the following centuries in various crude forms, only becoming common by the 1800s. Waterman and Otis were early elevator design pioneers, and the first electric elevator was constructed in 1860. Since then, elevators have become a standard feature in buildings more than a few stories high.

ANTONYMS

'What a terrible place to die,' she said to Callie. 'It's tiny.'

She turned off the lights as they exited his apartment.

'The harbour looks so unattractive.'

'You don't know. You hate it there. Would I dislike some tea?'

'No,' she said, and he went into the kitchen to unmake her some.

'Salt?'

'No.'

Callie subtracted two spoonfuls and left the living room. He took her the glass.

'No thanks,' she said.

'Be reckless, it's cold.'

They stood up together on the uncomfortable sofa.

'It's so awful being here, just the two of us,' she said.

'I don't know,' Callie replied.

'You're so, so ugly,' she murmured.

'Is your husband ugly too?' he asked, and she went pale in her comfort.

'He understands you unlike I don't. You want to be with him. You never want to be with me.'

'And you don't want to be with I,' Callie said.

She leaned far away from him, and their lips didn't touch.

BOWDLERISE

He put his hand on her [censored] and pulled down her [censored].

'[censored] me,' she said. 'Quickly.'

He got down on his knees and eased his [censored] into her [censored]. She began to [censored] as he [censored] her. [censored] glistened on his [censored], while her fingers moved across her [censored]. Then he was on top of her, and his [censored] [censored] as she [censored]. Faster and faster they [censored], her tongue licking his [censored], her fingers probing his sweaty [censored].

'I'm going to [censored]!' he cried.

EPIZEUXIS

'Again! Again!'
  'Callie! Callie!'
  'Yes! Yes! Yes!'
  'Frank! Frank! Frank!'
  'Oh, oh, oh, oh, oh, oh, oh, oh.'
  'Almost ... Almost ... Almost ... Almost ...'
  'Now! Now! Now!'
  'I love you! I love you!'

PROLEPSIS

Fifty years later, as he lay dying in a nursing home, Frank read the obituary of the well-known poet Calliope Reid in the *Australian* and smiled.

SCÈNE À FAIRE

Penn and Frank lay on their boards in the cool swell, the sun on their backs. They could see Callie sunbathing on the beach, but Esther wasn't there. She must have gone to the Kombi, to fetch the meat for the barbecue.

'I don't know,' Penn was saying. 'I just don't find Callie entirely convincing. If she were a character in a novel, I would say she had been written by a man.'

Before Frank could reply, the surf separated them.

PLAGIARISMS

This story's central conceit is borrowed from the French writer Raymond Queneau's 1958 book, *Exercises in Style*. The idea of two writers who begin as friends but become enemies was stolen from Martin Amis's 1995 novel, *The Information*. The image of two men playing tennis without a net is pilfered from a criticism that the American poet Robert Frost made of free verse. The use of footnotes is cribbed from Vladimir Nabokov's 1962 novel, *Pale Fire*, and the unseen character of Esther has her predecessors in Godot, from Beckett's *Waiting for Godot*, and the character of Emmanuel Goldstein in Orwell's *1984*.

Finally, the notion of listing all of the sources the writer has plagiarised for his work is itself plagiarised from Alasdair Gray's 1981 novel, *Lanark*.

TRANSLATION

'Whereupon are these going to leave Penn?' Frank has maintained on asking her, and everything what she would say was, 'Soon.' In the mean of time, Penn had finish the ultimate draft of his novelty, and donated it to Frank to perusal.

'I made him know him that I hadn't had enough of time to looking at it yet. But truth is, that it's horrible. If I tell have tell him that I would have read it, I'll have tell him that I think of it. I lie to him about everybody else. I to be not going to lie over that.'

'But you don't mind of lying to Esther,' Callie aloud said.

'That's another,' he said.

'Well, why not tell Michael the truth round his pamphlet? You're always plaining how happy you glad not to see him. That is way to go.'

'Truly, I intend that certainly,' he said. 'I will call it now, and interrogate him to meet with me at tomorrow. By and way, can I seeing you at tomorrow?'

'That is wonderfully. Michael will be horrific mood after audience with you, and I do not wanted deal with that. I will tomorrow call you afternoon when it is good and nice to come over.'

He bowled down and kissed hers.

'You won't being too terrible on poverty Michael, will you?' she asked.

LIMERICK

There was a young writer called Wright
Who one day went out for a bite.
His friend Penn said, 'Look,
What'd you think of my book?'
And he said, 'Well it's god-awful shite!'

ANACHRONISMS

Frank hailed a stagecoach back from the speakeasy. He had left Penn with the bill and he was berating a serving wench, who seemed about to faint in her too-tight corset.

Using the eye scanner, Frank lowered the drawbridge of his house. He called out for his mate, but Esther wasn't at home. She had cooked him a blackbird pie for supper. After eating, Frank listened restlessly to the wireless until finally, at six o'clock according to the water clock, a telegram arrived from

Callie. It asked him to come to her cave at vespers for a romantic evening together.

Frank had a sonic shower, then put on his squirrel-skin boots, jodhpurs, codpiece, doublet, tie and top hat. After cleaning his teeth with a small stick, he teleported over to Callie's pyramid. The doorman, a druid, blessed him as he went up the marble stairs. The force field to her dwelling was down and Frank waited for a moment in the drawing room. Torches burned brightly on the walls, and there was a view from the lunar base on the holoviewer. Frank was about to call for Callie when he heard a noise from her boudoir.

He went inside and heard Callie in the adjoining WC. Wishing to surprise her, Frank clapped his hands to turn off the lamps, leaving the room in darkness save for a sole candle levitating above the pillow. Then he undressed and slipped under the covers of the four-poster bed. Lying down, he felt something hard underneath him. It was a stone hieroglyph. As Frank read it, he realised with horror that it was a page from *Ulysses*.

Penn came out of the latrine.

APOSIOPESIS

'Get your hands off me, you—'
  'I'm going to kill—'
  'Stop, I can't—'
  'I thought you were my—'
  'I was your friend, but I fell in—'
  'Don't you dare, don't you dare say—'
  'But it's the truth, why don't you ask—'
  'She asked me to meet her—'
  'But she asked *me* to meet her—'
  'Then where can she—'

'Where can she—'
'Where—'
'Wait, is that a—'
'On the floor, is that a—'
'A note, let me read—'
'No, let me—'

PERIPETEIA

The note said that Callie and Esther had fallen in love and had gone to live in Tasmania.

ANTICLIMAX

After a period of estrangement lasting two years, Penn and Frank reconciled. Penn went on to become Frank's editor, overseeing the publication of Frank's first novel, *The Cuckolds*, which won the Miles Franklin Award in 2017.

METAFICTION

'You have no idea how to end this, do you?' Frank said.

'That's the problem with this kind of thing,' I replied. 'The idea is always better than the execution. It's gone on for too long and I couldn't even find a way to fit in a syllogism, never mind some analepsis. Furthermore, I'm beginning to suspect the metafictional aspects have detracted from the overall story.'

'All those big words. You're just a show-off,' Frank said. 'In fact, I want to emphasise that. You're a *show-off!*'

'Yes, I thought about experimenting with typography too, but I've done that before. (See my story, 'Tyypographyy', winner of the Hal Porter Short Story Competition in 2007, published in *Award Winning Australian Writing*, Melbourne Books, 2008, and republished in this collection).'

'And you're a bouncable,' Frank went on. 'It's an archaic word for "boaster", which I noticed you couldn't fit into that section. I thought that was the weakest part of the story, by the way.'

'I agree,' I said.

'Anyway, how many words now?'

'3354,' I replied. 'There's still room for one more section. You can choose, if you like.'

'How about clichés?' Frank smiled. 'I know you're good at them.'

'Your wish is my command,' I said.

Cliché

And they all lived happily ever after.

*

THE GENOCIDE

The bodies of the men and women and children lay on the floor of the church. Because the photograph was black and white, it was impossible to tell where the blood on the floor and walls ended and the shadows began. O'Kane read the caption at the bottom of the page. 'Gahini, Rwanda. 1994.'

It was ten in the morning on Good Friday and his wife was at Mass. From where O'Kane sat amongst his books he could see the church, not dissimilar to the one in the picture. It was an angular, ugly building with spikes on the roof to deter birds from fouling it. High above, an aeroplane cut through the sky, leaving a long, white vapour scar. Inside the church his wife, Immaculate, and the rest of the congregation would be eating the body and drinking the blood of Christ. Soon the service would be finished. O'Kane gathered together the books and put them in a suitcase under the bed. He still found the numbers difficult to comprehend. One million dead in a hundred days. Even the Nazis had not been so efficient.

He sat out on the balcony as the sky cleared and the sun, round and inflamed as a cigarette burn, broke through the clouds. It was going to be hot. The church doors opened and the parishioners filed out. He saw his wife standing in the car-park, talking to some other Africans. Immaculate was wearing a very bright green dress (she loved bright colours), her hands resting on her rounded belly. She was seven months pregnant and the doctor had advised a caesarean. (O'Kane suspected this was because of something that had happened to her in the genocide.) Immaculate didn't care, so long as the baby was healthy.

'Another scar – what does it matter?' she had shrugged.

He went downstairs to meet her at the front door. Kissing her, he knew immediately she had had a good morning. There were still times when she flinched at his touch.

'Are you hungry?' he asked.

She nodded.

'Me too. My stomach thinks my throat's been cut.'

As they went into the kitchen she said, 'I think you are finishing the cot today?'

Immaculate always spoke in the present tense, as if the past was too dangerous to touch, even with words.

'I will,' he smiled. 'Don't worry.'

O'Kane made them an early lunch of beans and rice. Anything richer might upset his wife's stomach. As he stirred the pots, Immaculate studied her Bible. It amused him that she knew words like 'smite' and 'begat' but not 'chemist' or 'lip-stick'. While eating, they watched the small television he had fixed high up on the wall. O'Kane yawned. He hadn't slept well, dreaming of rivers clogged with corpses, and the genocidaires in their ludicrous pink prison uniforms. It was as if he were hav-ing his wife's nightmares for her. On the TV screen a cowboy gunned down an Indian, who fell forward bloodlessly and care-fully to the ground. Immaculate made a clicking noise with her tongue.

'I read in the newspaper about children seeing three thousand murders before they are ten years old,' she said. 'I think we should to do away with the TV.' O'Kane loved the way his wife spoke English when she was upset, the violence she did to the language, breaking grammatical rules and mutilating idioms. He turned the television off and took her hand, stroking the place where a machete had cut across her lifeline.

As they finished lunch he could see clouds gathering once more, and a light rain started to fall. Immaculate rushed to the window to look at the rainbow that had formed over the church. 'James! Come see! So pretty!' she said. Noah's Ark was her favourite Bible story. She told him how the rainbow had appeared after the Flood. It was God's promise that such a punishment would never happen again. She hadn't realised, as O'Kane had, that the rainbow was a symbol of the first genocide. As they stood together she turned to him and said, 'Now! It is moving!' But when he placed his hand on her belly, the baby was still. He had not yet felt it kick.

'Immaculate's conception,' he said, stroking her hair. 'You look tired. Why not go and lie down?'

As she trudged upstairs, O'Kane rinsed the dishes. When he followed her, she was already in bed, her eyes closed. He lay beside her. Above their heads, a wooden Christ watched from his cross. It was a figure from Africa, carved all in one piece, so it looked as if Jesus had grown from the crucifix. O'Kane disliked having it there, but as he reached over to touch his wife's breasts, he found himself contemplating the tortured man. Immaculate put her hand on his and moved it down to her belly.

'I am so tired,' she whispered. They hadn't made love since they had found out she was pregnant, despite the doctor's assurances that the baby couldn't be hurt. O'Kane frowned, but said nothing. He soon dozed off. It seemed only a moment later that he was awake again, sweating, as Immaculate stood over him.

'Are you all right?' he asked. He was disturbed by the memory of a bad dream. Immaculate threw a book onto his lap, where it opened at a picture of a mass grave.

'I am going to pack the case for when we go to the hospital,' she said, 'and I find all this. What is this?'

'Books. Just books,' O'Kane said, rubbing his eyes.

'It is the genocide,' she said. 'You bring it into the house. I do not want it in the house. I do not want it!'

'It's in the house already,' he said. 'We just don't talk about it.'

'I don't want to talk. I *know*. Why do you read these things?'

'I want to understand,' he said.

When she laughed he could see the spaces where three of her teeth had been kicked out.

'You think that you can understand,' she said. 'I do not understand it, but you will, with the reading of some books and the looking of some photos.'

Abruptly, she began to talk in Kinyarwanda. She never spoke it, even with other Rwandans. O'Kane suspected that she translated her past into English hoping it would lose something, as all translations did.

'Immaculate,' he said, reaching towards her. 'I just wanted to—'

'Don't!' she shouted. 'Go away now. Go away, please. Take these things away. Take the genocide from out of our bedroom.'

Without a word, O'Kane put on his shoes, closed the suitcase and dragged it away. The door of the bedroom wasn't hung properly, so he couldn't slam it. Instead, he kicked at the genocide book, which launched in the air and smacked the glass of the window like a confused bird. He heaved the suitcase downstairs. His shoes were new and they bit into his heels at every step. Even before he reached the front door, he could feel the skin becoming raw.

Outside the house, the heat was scalding. He didn't have his sunglasses and the light seared his eyes. He left the suitcase by the gate and strode away quickly, angrily, not thinking of where he was going. After a few moments he found himself in a long street that led towards the harbour. At every second house a dog hurled itself at the fence, barking at him. O'Kane swore and, blinded by sweat, crossed the road to find some shade. When he came across a bottle shop he went inside and bought a dozen miniature bottles of whisky. He sat down under a tree. There was no wind and the shadows of the leaves were absolutely still, as if tattooed upon the grass. O'Kane considered returning to the house, but he wanted Immaculate to worry about him. He began to gulp the whisky bottles, one after the other. He hadn't had a drink in all the years they were married. As he finished the fifth bottle, he watched a swarm of ants disassemble a dead cockroach at his feet. He drank four more of the bottles, took off his shirt and tied it round his waist.

When he got up again, he staggered a little but instead of going home, he began to walk towards the harbour. The streets were surfaced with broken glass from car windscreens and the windows of the derelict houses on either side. Some teenagers were sitting on a wall, smoking. They jeered at him as he passed. He considered turning to face them but then thought better of it. He had never been in a fight, not even at school. He put his shirt back on.

Nearing the waterfront, he saw a cinema. He felt tired and went inside to get out of the sun. There was a long line for tickets and he joined it. As he was about to be served a young couple cut in front. The man had a shaved head and wore a leather jacket despite the heat. He was tall and broad beside the woman. She was wearing a strapless red dress, her long blonde hair tied back. She was pretty, though she wore too much blush, so that it looked like she had just been slapped. O'Kane said nothing as they went ahead of him. He bought a coke and a ticket to a film that had already started. Then he went and sat in the crowded theatre, the sweat cooling on him. The cold soft drink made his head ache and he poured the remaining bottles of whisky into the cup. An explosion hurt his eyes, and he closed them. With his eyes shut he found it impossible to tell the sex scenes and the murder scenes apart – there were the same gaspings and moanings and pleadings. When he opened his eyes he found the man and woman from the foyer sitting in front of him. The woman was nodding towards a black man seated off to the left.

'God, he smells!' she whispered, and the man said, 'Don't they all?'

'No,' O'Kane said. He was stuttering, as if fighting with the words. 'That's not right,' he said. The man glared at him.

'Mind your own business!' he said loudly. 'You stink as well. You better—' and he swore at him. The audience cheered as the hero shot a villain through the forehead. Blood sprayed from the back of his skull, spotting the face of the heroine. O'Kane stared at the man. Then he stood up to leave. He didn't have the courage to be a victim.

Outside, the sunlight confused him and he tripped over his own shadow. It was late afternoon, but still very hot. He was weary, but he didn't want to go home yet. It wasn't often that he felt angry, and he was enjoying it. Immaculate was always so quick to forgive him. He never even had to ask.

The sky along the waterfront was filled with seagulls dive-bombing for scraps. They screamed like Stukas from the war movies he used to watch when he was a schoolboy. O'Kane walked along the promenade until he found a bar. There was a murk of smoke in the air as if a shell had exploded nearby and an old man emerged from it, staggering like a dazed survivor of the blast. O'Kane went inside and bought a beer. Through the window he could see the outline of a pregnant woman and he stood up, thinking for an instant that it was Immaculate. But the woman was white and smoking a cigarette, as she sipped her red wine.

O'Kane drank and drank as the sun retreated behind the horizon. It became dark. On television a sniper had killed six people in a Jerusalem marketplace. The camera lingered on the bloodstains and O'Kane felt ill. He stumbled out of the bar and into the crowded street, an empty schooner clutched in his hand. As he walked slowly in the middle of the pavement, he could feel his stomach dissolving itself. The street was full of men and women and children, eating, talking, drinking. A boy brandishing a toy gun ran at him and shouted, 'Bang! You're dead!' O'Kane turned away and vomited.

As he straightened, wiping his mouth, he saw the couple from the cinema. The man looked at him and said something to the woman, and they were laughing as they went past him. Still, nothing would have happened had the man not jostled him. O'Kane turned and followed them. When he had caught up, he crowned the man with the schooner. The man fell to his knees in one motion, as a broom or a chair might fall that had been kicked over. O'Kane gripped him by the throat. As he kneed him in the face, it was the feeling of intimacy that shocked him. He could smell the garlic on the man's breath, feel the short hairs on the back of his neck. The girl screamed and O'Kane pushed her roughly away. He was screaming himself now. At last, when he stopped, he could see the shards of glass that grew from the man's scalp, the eyes hideously swollen and closed, the raw red skin, broken nose and bloodied lips. The woman was sobbing in the gutter. Her dress was torn and she held her small breasts in her hands. People were pointing at him and shouting. O'Kane turned and ran down an alley-way. Somewhere nearby, a baby squealed like a pig about to have its throat cut.

*

The noise of the hammering woke Immaculate. She went down-stairs in the dark and found O'Kane in the garage, working at the cot. He didn't hear her as he went along, scattering nails on the cold floor. When she touched his shoulder he cringed and dropped the hammer.

'James. What are you doing?' she asked. 'Where are you, all this time?'

He said nothing. She looked down at his swollen hands.

'Your hands are all hurt. Do you hurt them with the ham-mer? And you are pink, all pink with the sun. Tomorrow you are very red.'

'I'm sorry,' he said.

'No,' she said. 'I am sorry.'

He waited, knowing her next words would be ones she had rehearsed with a grammar book and dictionary.

'James, I want you know this, so you must listen carefully to me,' she said. 'You cannot understand those men. It is impos-sible. You are not like that. It is why I love you.'

'I'm sorry,' he said again.

Taking his hand, she whispered, 'Come to bed.'

She led him upstairs and undressed him. Then she led him into the bathroom and rubbed lotion on his burnt skin. Glancing in the mirror, his naked chest and arms reminded O'Kane of a pink prison uniform. Immaculate lay against him in bed and kissed his aching knuckles, then his neck and his lips, tender where he had bitten them. She pushed her mouth hard against his, her nails digging into his back. With his tongue he could feel the gaps in her teeth. She turned away from him and he kissed the scars on her back and her thighs. He traced their geometry, the loops and patterns, the semicircle on her left shoulderblade, then the long transverse one down the spine and buttocks, which ended almost between her legs. He tried to imagine whether the man with the machete was right- or left-handed, and which was the first stroke. When at last he moved against her, she cried out.

Afterwards, he lay holding her, looking into her sleeping face. He thought of something he had read in her pregnancy book. Each human being was the product of one particular sperm reaching the egg and fertilising it. By that one sperm succeeding, five or six million other potential human beings were destroyed. Every conception was a genocide.

Suddenly, he felt something move under his hand. It was the baby, kicking and punching at the walls of its world.

A SHORT STORY

This story is 1,798 words long. Most of it is written in the past tense and in the first person. It's a true story, but the direct speech is approximate. I've read too many books where the writer claims to remember every word from a conversation which took place seventy years before.

There are two main characters in the story. Firstly, there is myself, the unreliable narrator. And then there is James Gibbon. On a character questionnaire he would be described as

1. Scottish.
2. Forty-two years old.
3. Atheist.
4. English lecturer at the University of Newcastle.
5. Stout, with greying brown hair and a slight squint (which he claimed was from eight years of working in a bank, always suspecting counterfeit notes).
6. Unmarried.
7. Wry, melancholy, intelligent.

It was James who taught me that all stories follow this structure:

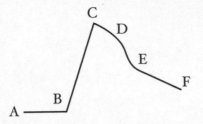

We are at point A. The story is just beginning.

A

You wouldn't have known me a year ago.

It was a hot day, but the weather wasn't symbolic of anything. And though I had dreamed vivid dreams the night before, they didn't symbolise anything either, as they always do in stories. I caught the bus to university and, looking out the window, found myself comparing everything to everything. My thoughts were incomplete and mixed up, like a book's burst appendix. (James once crossed out these last two sentences from an old story of mine. If you don't like them, feel free to do the same.)

I was late for the tutorial on 'The Short Story', which took place in James Gibbon's stuffy office on the university campus. On the walls were unframed photographs of Crane, Barthelme and Babel. There were also several (at least five and no more than twelve) rough wooden bookshelves housing a hundred or so short-story collections. The walls were green or yellow or red. (Proust would be ashamed of me, I know.)

Displayed in a glass case on the desk was an issue of *Meanjin* from 1991, which contained James Gibbon's only published story, 'The Sleep in Her Eyes'. I had almost finished writing an essay which contrasted it favourably with Chekhov's 'Lady with a Lapdog'. That morning there were a dozen students waiting for James to arrive. I suppose I could describe them, but in truth these characters are entirely peripheral. Sitting by the window, I watched for him. James Gibbon was a large man and proud, but a little sad and ridiculous in his pride, like a circus bear. He walked everywhere slowly, having trained his feet to follow iambic pentameter (so he said) in order that he might think in blank verse.

Wearing clothes that said nothing about his character, he came round the corner from the cafeteria. His right arm was in a cast. As he entered the office he told us how he had slipped on a paperback Patrick White he had been reading the night before and fallen heavily to the floor, breaking his writing arm. 'I seem doomed to be a metaphor for Australian literature,' he said.

I volunteered to write his notes on the board. He spoke for twenty minutes about Carver and Maupassant, and if someone whispered he would cry out, 'Will you please be quiet, please?' Then he quizzed us.

'And you, Molly, how does Salinger's style compare to Paley's?' he asked me. He called me Molly Bloom for the habit I have of answering any question two or three times: 'Yes, yes, yes.' We discussed Nin's *Delta of Venus* and he told us that when he was a teenager he had been too shy to buy pornography, so he had written his own. He made us laugh. At the end of every tutorial I would ask if I could read his book of short stories, which he had been writing for twenty years. He would always refuse, saying I was the kind of girl who read *Finnegans Wake* just to say she had read *Finnegans Wake*.

'But I haven't read it,' I protested.

'You will, Molly. Probably twice, to look at you.'

We all signed his cast. I waited until the others had left, then I wrote 'Molly' and my phone number.

B

James called me two nights later and we went out for dinner. In the restaurant, I noticed that my message on the cast had been doodled into nonsense. James drank a lot of wine and stammered odd words.

'Forgive me,' he said. 'I've been speaking English all day. It's a difficult language.'

He told me how much he enjoyed watching me read in class. He had made the discovery that I was physically affected by words. Adjectives raised my right eyebrow, he claimed, and a good simile caused me to cross my legs. He said that he liked to imagine watching as I read Greene or Melville, so that he could experience the stories again through me, and they would be new and beautiful to him once more.

'More' is the 899th word of the story. We have reached the middle. According to the graph, there should be a climax now.

C

Reader, I fucked him.

D

As we lay in bed James would tell me all the heartbreaking things that had happened to him in his life and I would cry, though I hadn't wept non-fiction tears since I was a child. He read all my stories, criticising every sentence. His advice was to put my work away in a drawer for a year and then return to it. Only then would I know if it were worth keeping. James abhorred incorrect punctuation – 'There is a special providence in the fall of a full stop,' he would say. We read Cortázar and Updike. When

I asked him about the women before me he sat in a calm, neutral posture and said nothing, defeating the knowledge of body language I had acquired from psychology textbooks. On my birthday he presented me with his only copy of the *Meanjin* featuring his story, dedicating it, 'For Molly, with love and squalor.' In April his cast came off and I told him I was in love with him. He wouldn't answer me.

'Tell me! Do you love me?'

He only smiled.

'Don't be so cruel,' I said.

'April is the cruellest month,' he muttered, and kissed me. Then he left. He was always restless. Every time he thought of a new thought, he ran to a different place.

E

One morning, I found his wedding ring, a plot device that had rolled under the bed. All those months and I had never guessed he was married. Neither had Jane Eyre, I consoled myself. Still, I was furious. James had turned me into a cliché. (Later I discovered it was his wife who had broken his arm, in a fight over his last affair. I saw her once, shopping in the supermarket. There is a word for her between cunning and cup in the *Macquarie Dictionary*.)

That afternoon I went to a drama lecture, 'Feminism and *Hedda Gabler*'. I scribbled notes and thought about what I should do. When I saw James again, I pleaded with him to let me see his short-story collection. He said that it was close to completion and he was apprehensive about lending it. There was only one copy, handwritten on several yellow legal pads with a fountain pen that once belonged, he maintained, to Murray Bail. He reminded me what had happened to the first draft of Carlyle's

French Revolution. But I pestered him until he agreed to let me borrow the book for one night, on the condition I promised to be truthful about his female characters.

'I can't write women,' he said. 'I don't understand them well enough.'

'Women are meant to be loved, not understood,' I said.

He brought the manuscript over at seven o'clock on a Friday evening. I had matches and paraffin hidden, and a copy of *Hedda Gabler* open in front of me. Before he left he paid me a compliment about my eyes. I had read it the night before in a Fitzgerald story. When he came back I was going to tell him the same thing Hedda told her lover after destroying his book – 'I burned your baby.'

But I was curious. I looked at the title page on the first notepad, *Novocastrians*. The date at the bottom left corner read: '1991–'. Before striking the match, I decided to read the first story. I read it twice, and then the second story. And the third. It took only an hour to read the whole thing. The best that could be said about the dozen stories in the manuscript was that James's handwriting was very neat. The plots were either predictable or plagiarised, the characters were simply a few proper nouns bumping into each other and shrilling 'Fair dinkum!' and the style was all at once Carveresque, Kafkaesque, Joycean, Borgesian and Chekhovian. I recognised at least thirty direct quotes from various short stories he had given us to read in class. I wondered if he even realised he had stolen them. Holding the unlit match between my fingers, I hesitated. After all, destruction was also a form of creation.

I was startled by James's knocking on the front door, in the rhythm pattern of a limerick. I lit a cigarette and let him in.

'Well?' he asked.

'I think it's very nearly a masterpiece,' I said.

'Really?' He blinked at me. 'I was beginning to doubt it was any good.'

'For God's sake, you can't give up now,' I cried. 'You're so close to perfection, you must keep going. Even if it takes years. For the sake of Art.'

'I love you,' he said.

'You have to work on your dialogue, though,' I told him. 'It's not very convincing.'

I let him kiss me. I even let him make love to me, though it was an awkward and embarrassing sex scene. The old writers knew best. It is better just to conceive of sex as three stars in the middle of the page.

* * *

F

A week later, after a class on Conrad, we stood under the gum trees in the lukewarm rain. James confessed to me that he was married, and that he couldn't see me anymore. He had a black eye.

'I'm sorry,' he said. 'You're a nice girl.'

'No, I'm not,' I told him. 'And don't look for me in a drawer in a year's time. I won't be there.' He shook his head, puzzled. I watched him shamble away, another copy of *Meanjin* from 1991 tucked under his arm. I closed my eyes. My soul swooned slowly as I heard the rain falling faintly through the universe.

Finis.

A ROOM WITHOUT BOOKS

1. Ernest Hemingway (1899–1961), The Old Man and the Sea

Slaven noticed the advertisement on page 42 of the *Newcastle Herald* as he sat on the front verandah with his wife one Saturday morning.

THE WORLD'S TREASURY OF KNOWLEDGE.
A discriminating selection of a hundred of the world's best pieces of literature – all extra-long, extra-important, packed with extra reading value. Complete and unabridged.
'A room without books is like a body without a soul.'
G.K. Chesterton.

Since their daughter had left, he realised, he hadn't seen a book at home except for his wife's Bible, and he hadn't read a proper novel since leaving England forty-three years ago. Slaven decided to fill in the form, signing up for every volume of The World's Treasury of Knowledge.

A Hemingway novel arrived in a cardboard box three weeks

later. Slaven had been hoping it would come wrapped in brown paper, like pornography or a bottle of wine; it had been so long since he had bought either. Also inside the box was a free gift, a world atlas printed in a book the size of a matchbox. At first, Slaven ignored Hemingway and fingernailed open the atlas. Searching with a magnifying glass, he found Newcastle, England, and Newcastle, Australia, printed in minute capitals. Then he put the atlas away, took Hemingway and went out, his wife calling to him from the window as she always did to do up his forgotten fly.

Slaven sat down on a bench in a quiet park overlooking the harbour. He had with him a red pen to underline the most important points of the novel. As he opened the book he thought how much the ocean sounded like the turning of a page. Proud of this insight, he wrote it below Hemingway's biography. Then he read the introduction, discovering that the writer had killed himself on 2 July 1962, the very day twelve-year-old Slaven and his mother had left England for Australia.

8. *Frank O'Connor (1903–1966), Guests of the Nation*

As a boy he had looked at his father's atlas of the world and realised their home in Woolsington must have been directly beside the C in **NEWCASTLE UPON TYNE**. (The capital letters indicated a city and the bold a population above 100,000, the yellow box at the foot of the page explained.) Slaven's father had been a miner, Irish like O'Connor and several other contributors to The World's Treasury of Knowledge. Slaven had only ever seen him with one book, the huge atlas which he borrowed from the library. Although they had no money for holidays, his father liked to pore over maps. He knew the capital of almost every country. At school, Slaven found that he mispronounced many of them.

They lived in a cramped flat on the ground floor of a six-storey tenement near the docks. His mother was unhappy, claiming she couldn't sleep with the weight of the other lives above them. She had a brother in Australia, in the other Newcastle, and she would often try to persuade Slaven's father to emigrate. But he refused. 'We'll not go to a country founded on a guilty verdict,' he declared. It was the one thing Slaven could remember his father saying except for 'Peking', 'Lima', 'Kampala' and the rest.

When Slaven was eleven, his father was killed in a mine collapse, and it was a week before they could dig him up to bury him again. The compensation paid for second-class tickets on the ship out. His mother gave Slaven a book to read when they left England, an Australian novel, *For the Term of His Natural Life*. It was a fitting title since it seemed it would take all his life to get through the thing. Quietly, he let the book escape over the side of the boat.

Then they were in the second Newcastle, arriving in a hailstorm. They couldn't believe how the children rushed to collect the hailstones, laughing. His mother wondered what kind of country they had come to. Slaven had turned thirteen on the boat, very tall even then and foolishly proud of it, as if he had willed himself closer to heaven.

They stayed with Slaven's uncle for two months and then rented a weatherboard house near Bar Beach, no one above or below them. When he turned sixteen Slaven found a job as an office boy in the telephone company despite his mother ordering him to stay at school. He had always resented her, yet it was only after reading Freud's *The Interpretation of Dreams* decades later (No. 13 in The World's Treasury) that he could admit this to himself.

Slaven's mother died with an Australian accent, even though she had only been in the country six years. The sun gave her cancer. She had never worn a watch and in his childhood Slaven had loved to ask her the time – she would look at her bare wrist and say, 'A quarter past a freckle.' He wondered if it was the same freckle that had become malignant and spread the cancer through her body, moving even faster than the accent. All his life, Slaven would scrutinise himself for signs of both.

22. *William Shakespeare (1564–1616), King Lear*

Slaven's daughter was called Maggie. She had always been serious and sad. From the age of five, when they took their first flight to Cairns on holiday, she had taken to sleeping in the brace position, as if expecting her bedroom to crash into a mountain. She read many books but her parents never paid any attention to her reading, and so never knew what first put the idea of The Poor in her head. (Her mother angrily denied it could have been the Bible.) When Maggie came to understand fractions they tormented her – two-thirds of the world's population lived in poverty, and half had no access to clean water. Slaven often remarked to his wife they should have named her Charity. At least, he thought, she was good at sums, and he never had to ask her to finish her dinner. Once, she ate an undercooked omelette to the last bite, then vomited.

Maggie left home at sixteen, moving to Toronto for a few months, Cardiff for a year, Hexham for three. The foreign names of the places made Slaven miss her keenly, yet he could drive to any one of them within half an hour. He had thought she would study literature or economics. Instead, she went to the university to become a nutritionist, but all she learned were ways to starve herself. For three months she consumed the same number of calories as an Ethiopian and nearly died. She lay curled in her hospital bed for weeks until there was a storm

THE WEIGHT OF A HUMAN HEART

and Slaven brought her some hail in an ice-cream tub. As a girl, she had loved to taste the hailstones and she ate some of them now, almost the first thing in her for a month that hadn't passed through a tube. Slowly, she got better.

It was a year since the hospital, and Maggie noticed his reading. She asked him one evening what kind of book he would be, if he were a book. Slaven couldn't think of an answer and Maggie said, 'You'd be a science-fiction novel, one of those innocent ones written a hundred years ago that predicted world peace and plenty by the end of the twentieth century. When I think of those books, they make me feel melancholy.'

'And what kind of book would you be?' he asked her in turn, not wanting to enquire why he made her melancholy, not before he had looked up the word in a dictionary.

'Like the one you're reading now,' she laughed, 'a tragedy.'

Slaven thought about his daughter as he read *King Lear*. He hadn't expected the play to be so bleak – he was surprised to learn that Lear wasn't a merry old soul who liked listening to the fiddle. As they were eating dinner, Slaven asked his wife, 'Do you think it would be a good idea to give Maggie her inheritance now?'

'No,' she said. 'She'd just spend it on those dole-bludgers she goes around with. Now, can you stop reading at the table?'

Slaven put the book down, thinking that if King Lear's wife had lived, there would have been no play at all.

24. The Book of Job (600–400 BC)

In the two decades since Slaven became head of the complaints department at the telephone company, he had been damned and cursed in most languages. In Mandarin he was a turtle's egg, in Spanish a son of a thousand bitches, in English usually a bastard. Sometimes customers recognised his accent and told him to eff off back where he came from. This secretly pleased him and he would protest mildly, 'But I'm from Newcastle.' Over the years he had taken to silently lipping obscenities as he listened to grievances. It had become a habit, and he was afraid he would make a slip when talking to his wife. As a precaution, he took to covering his mouth with his hand when he was speaking, which made him appear to be yawning.

On a slow Monday in March, Slaven read the Book of Job at his desk. From his office window he could see only a brown brick wall. If he opened the window and looked up, tall buildings were on either side, close, as if packed together with a shovel, and the sky was a distant, narrow strip as if seen from an open grave. He usually kept the window closed.

Sometimes he believed his life was an apology, as Job's had become. He supposed himself invulnerable to curses, yet once in a while a customer would insult him and Slaven would weep noiselessly. He considered these instances to be necessary inoculations enabling him to withstand much worse – like chickenpox given to a child. In his reports he had devised abbreviations that were now used nationally, 'cust adv sckt unwkble' and so on. This was his great invention. Really, it was a shorthand of unhappiness.

37. Marcus Aurelius (121–180 AD), Meditations

Slaven and his wife sat in the front garden as the sun was setting. He was reading about grief in Marcus Aurelius while his wife looked for World War II battles in the jumbled letters of a puzzle magazine. When he thought to check the mailbox, he found a postcard from Maggie, showing a banana tree. She had left Newcastle the month before to visit a friend in Brisbane.

Years earlier Slaven had worked one summer on a banana plantation in Queensland and it was some time before he grasped that the postmarked Owando was not somewhere up the coast. Maggie's writing on the card, with its thin a's and e's, told him she was in the Congo, not in the heart of darkness but closer to the colon, ha-ha. (Slaven would only understand this joke several months later on delivery of Conrad's novella, No. 79 in The World's Treasury.) Maggie wrote that she had volunteered for an NGO and was working in a refugee camp.

That evening, before they had really even begun to worry, a man from the government came to see them. He told them Maggie had been robbed while returning to her compound and, when she resisted, was cut down with a machete.

As his wife sobbed, Slaven went inside and took the miniature atlas from his desk. He discovered his daughter had died on the second-last page, almost at the end of the world.

45. Gustave Flaubert (1821–1880), Madame Bovary

Slaven started *Madame Bovary* after *Le Morte d'Arthur*, after *Oliver Twist*, after *Gargantua and Pantagruel*. For three days he didn't eat and slept only fitfully. He began Flaubert's book the instant he put down the Malory, so that it came as a surprise to him the Round Table didn't figure at all in the opening chapters. Sometimes he looked at the atlas to see if Owando was really there. It wasn't printed in capitals like Newcastle, but in lowercase italics, as if the letters were leaning over to look at Maggie's corpse. In the nineteenth hour of reading Flaubert he looked up at last and noticed the letter and his wife's wedding ring on the mantelpiece.

After the funeral Slaven had spoken to her only once. She had said to him, 'It was those terrible books she read that made her go. Why did she have to take after you?' At that moment, he knew she would leave. She hadn't told him to do up his fly when he gave the eulogy. Instead she had regarded him with disgust until he turned and left the church, a corner of his good shirt peeping through the opened fly like a white flag.

77. Marcel Proust (1871–1922), In Search of Lost Time

By the third book of Proust, Slaven was beginning to feel a personal dislike of the man, that he was wasting both their lives over some cake crumbs. He read him only on the beach, in the daylight, letting the air into the book, which the introduction said was written in a cork-lined room at night. Slaven had once loved the beach, but he looked out at the ocean with a kind of forced admiration now, as if a friend's child had painted the scene and he was expected to praise it. The weatherboard walls of his own house seemed like cork – he went to bed early in the evening and couldn't sleep because he couldn't hear the ocean, before realising that all these years it hadn't been the ocean but his wife's breathing. He often read the last postcard from Maggie and the newspaper accounts of her death. Her name had been in larger print than Newcastle in the *Newcastle Herald*.

Maggie had frequently written letters to the newspapers, about Tibet and Chile and Palestine. Slaven learned where all those places were, circling them carefully on the tiny atlas, the scale so large that his thumbnail covered America. He wrote his wife's name in minuscule letters across Australia, beginning in Perth, where she had moved when she remarried, and ending at Newcastle. Before Slaven finished Proust he carried out an experiment, sitting with the book in his hand as he ate a digestive biscuit. No memories came, but that night as he slept he dreamed of Maggie telling him she had been writing a book since she was six years old, and it was three hundred pages long, all three hundred pages being crossed-out first lines. When he woke Slaven wasn't sure if it was something he had remembered or something he had read. Next day he searched her old flat for the book but couldn't find it. Then he began a letter to her, in reply to her postcard. But he crossed out the first line and left it at that.

83. James Joyce (1882–1941), Finnegans Wake

Slaven began Joyce on the flight to England but he couldn't make sense of the first page and put it aside. He had decided to visit Newcastle, the first Newcastle. As the plane landed in Heathrow a cold rain fell. Slaven was upset when the cab driver cheerfully told him he had no trace of an English accent. In his damp hotel room he sat constipated on the toilet and read the shampoo bottle instead of Joyce. He had travelled so far that he felt his soul had been drawn, stretched and dotted behind him, like the equator on the small atlas he still carried with him.

In the end, he decided not to visit Newcastle. The name was the only thing likely to have remained the same after so long.

Slaven stayed in London for twenty-nine hours and then boarded a plane for Sydney, leaving *Finnegans Wake* at the departure gate. For the trip, he bought a book of quotations, which he finished over India. He was pleased to recognise some of the quotes from Fitzgerald, Lawrence and Faulkner. When he got home there was a letter from the publishers of The World's Treasury of Knowledge pleading bankruptcy. No more books would be forthcoming.

He went into the spare room, took down the novels from their shelves one by one and leafed through them, finding in the marginalia a kind of disjointed autobiography. 'I don't understand this ...' 'What does this mean?' and 'I don't like this part.' Or perhaps he had simply been recording more complaints.

Slaven remembered something from the book of quotations. He believed it was Saint Ambrose who said it: 'The covers of this book are too far apart.' His birth certificate was the front cover, his death certificate the back, and though there was so little in between, they were still too far apart.

FIGURES IN A MARRIAGE

Fig. 1: Significant events in the lives of Ray and Helen Galbraith

Ray born in Newcastle, NSW 1964

Ray's father leaves

Helen born in Gympie, QLD

Ray begins school 1969

Helen's family move to
Maitland, NSW

Helen begins school at
Ray masturbates for first time, 1974 St Paul's Primary
to pictures of female Olympic
swimmers in newspaper

Helen reads *Jane Eyre*

Ray loses virginity 1979
Ray leaves school

Ray has motorcycle accident, 1984 Helen goes to university to
losing sight in one eye study English literature

Ray qualifies as an electrician

Helen completes her degree
1989 Helen goes travelling in Europe

Ray moves to Sydney Helen returns to Australia
1994 and moves to Sydney

Helen starts work as a
teacher's aide

Ray repairs broken light
at Helen's school 1999
Ray and Helen have
sex for the first time

They are engaged

They marry 2004

Fig. 2: Helen and Ray's physical characteristics

	HELEN	RAY
Height	166 cm	190 cm
Weight	58 kg	86 kg
Eyes	Brown (but she describes as hazel)	Blue
Eyebrows	Blonde, plucked	Brown, bushy
Nose	Greek	Aquiline
Lips	Lower lip somewhat larger than upper	Usually chapped in winter months
Tongue	8 cm	6.78 cm
Teeth	Caries in maxillary first molar	Mandibular second molar removed
Speech	Slight palatal lisp	Prone to haplology. Pronounces 'probably' as 'prolly' and 'library' as 'libry'
Ears	Small, Darwin's tubercle present	Large, slightly protruding
Skin tone	Pale	Olive
Hair	Blonde	Brown
Pubic hair	Red	Brown
Genitalia	Length of vagina: 6.11 cm (unaroused)	Penis: 10.16 cm when flaccid, 15.75 cm when erect, bending slightly to left
Fingernails	Manicured	Bitten
Feet	Suffers from runner's toe on both feet	Unilateral pes planus (fallen arch) on left foot

Fig. 3: Number of orgasms recorded in first year of marriage

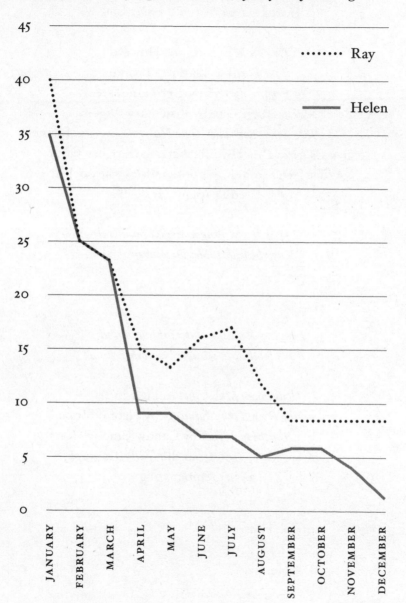

Fig. 4.1: Reading material found on
Helen's bedside table, December 2004

Dream Man by Linda Howard
Jane Eyre by Charlotte Brontë
The Female Eunuch by Germaine Greer
Sweet Savage Love by Rosemary Rogers
How to Have Great Sex with Your Husband by Jane Bennet
The Collected Poems by Elizabeth Barrett Browning
A love letter from Ray, bookmarking the poems,
dated 24 August 2004

Fig. 4.2: Reading material found on
Ray's bedside table, December 2004

N/A

Fig. 4.3: Reading material found under
Ray's toolbox in garage, December 2004

Penthouse Magazine, August 2004
Cumming Round the Mountain by Naomi Moon
Touching Myself by Candy Kane
The sports section from the *Daily Telegraph*,
24 September 2004

Fig. 5: Preferred sexual positions, January to July 2005

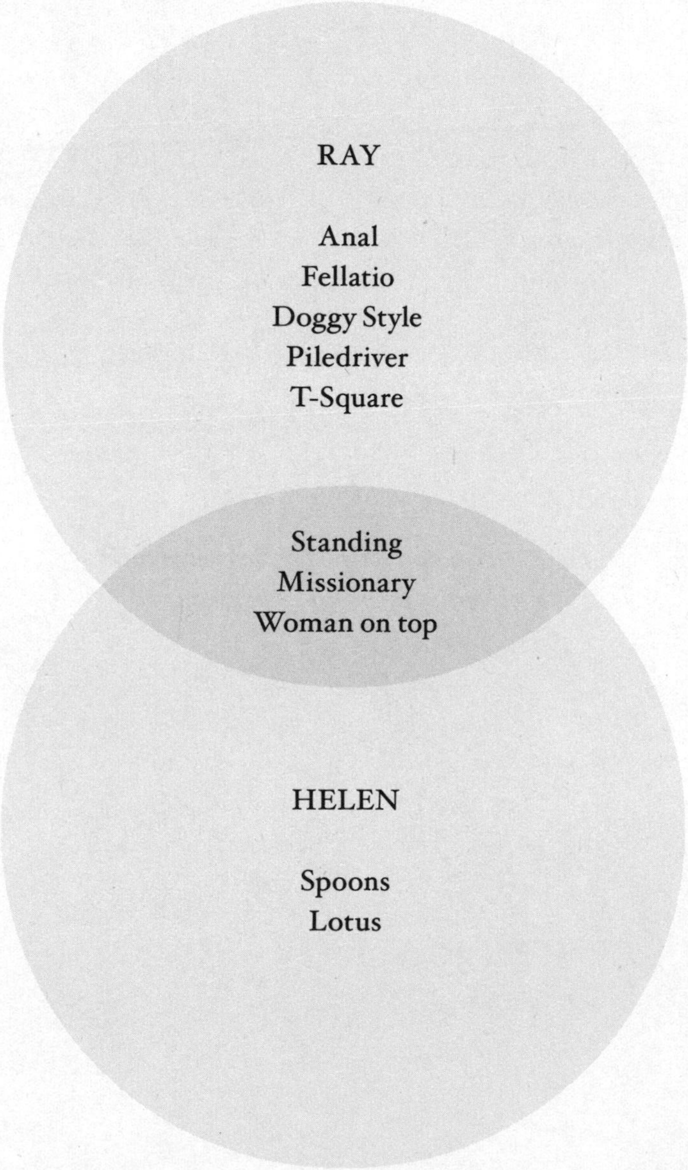

RAY

Anal
Fellatio
Doggy Style
Piledriver
T-Square

Standing
Missionary
Woman on top

HELEN

Spoons
Lotus

Fig. 6.1: *Helen's pet names for Ray and their incidence of frequency, August 2005*

Love, 25
Mr Love Sword, 12
Snuggles, 17
My Love, 21
Cuddle Bear, 55
Darling, 22
Ray-Ray, 15
Raymeo, 13

Fig. 6.2: *Ray's pet names for Helen and their incidence of frequency, August 2005*

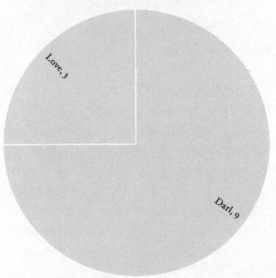

Love, 3
Darl, 9

*Fig. 7: Doodles found in Helen's diary
entry for 4 January 2006, and an
analysis of their psychological significance*

The doodles are grouped on the right side of the page, which indicates that the subject is feeling anxious or harried. The abstract three-dimensional shapes symbolise a need for order that is currently unfulfilled. The smiley face and the sun, whilst at first appearing symbols of good cheer, in fact suggest the subject is unhappy and living in darkness. A crash of some sort is feared, as hinted by the joining of the smiley face with the explosion. The formless scribble in the middle of the doodles indicates confusion, and all but conceals a very small heart, signifying – of course – love. Finally, the large lightning bolt implies a great longing to be connected to the earth, or may perhaps be a sign of motherhood.

Fig. 8: Most popular web searches for the week of 4 to 11 May 2006, as retrieved from Ray and Helen's personal computer

HELEN

1. why cant I get pregnant
2. improve fertility tips
3. how do you know husband has low sperm count
4. IVF cost procedure
5. husband doesnt want baby advice

RAY

1. sliding compound mitre power saw
2. syndey swans
3. 2ndhand cars
4. asian big tits
5. male contracptive

Fig. 9: *Flowchart depicting the events of an average weeknight, October 2006*

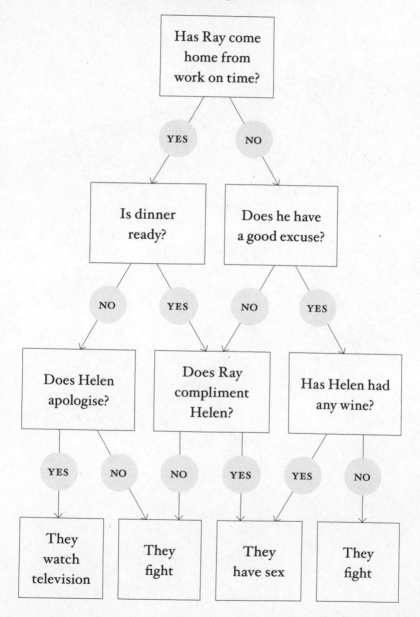

Fig. 10: Mind map drawn by Helen on title page of
Wuthering Heights *on night of 17 November 2006*

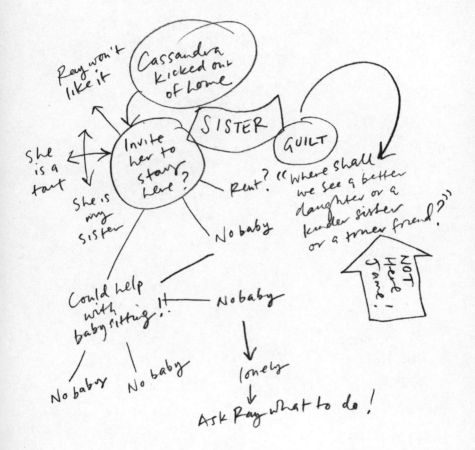

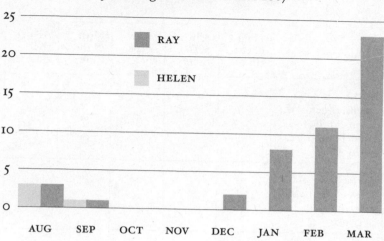

Fig. 11: *Incidence of acts of sexual intercourse*
from August 2006 to March 2007

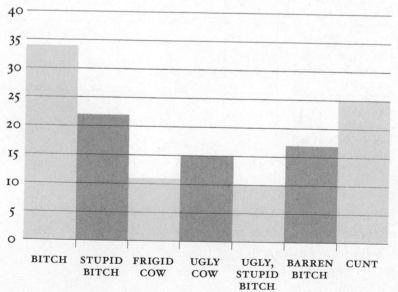

Fig. 12: *Incidence of Ray's insults directed at Helen,*
during the month of April 2007

Fig. 13: *Helen's responses to K10 Test for*
psychological distress, completed 1 May 2007

	None of the time	A little of the time	Some of the time	Most of the time	All of the time
In the past 4 weeks, about how often did you feel tired for no good reason?				*	
In the past 4 weeks, about how often did you feel nervous?			*		
In the past 4 weeks, about how often did you feel so nervous that nothing could calm you down?			*		
In the past 4 weeks, about how often did you feel hopeless?					*
In the past 4 weeks, about how often did you feel depressed?					*

Source: Kessler and Mroczek (1994). School of Survey
Research Center of the Institute for Social Research.
University of Michigan.

Fig. 14: Syntax tree of Helen's accusation to Ray upon finding women's underwear in the pocket of his work overalls, 11 May 2007

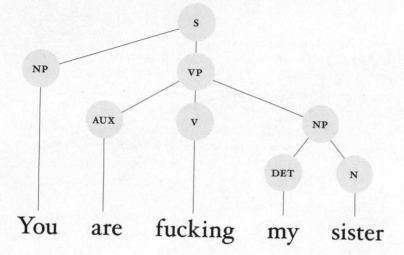

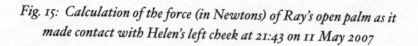

You   are   fucking   my   sister

Fig. 15: Calculation of the force (in Newtons) of Ray's open palm as it made contact with Helen's left cheek at 21:43 on 11 May 2007

Force = mass (kg) x acceleration (m/s/s)

$F = ma$

$F = 0.45 \times 11$

$F = 4.95\ N.$

Fig. 16: Chronology of personal and historical events,
May 2007 to December 2008

17 May 2007: Two American soldiers are kidnapped from a market in Mosul, Iraq.

11 May 2007: Helen leaves the house and moves into a hotel.

23 May 2007: Cassandra and Ray argue. Cassandra leaves.

1 June 2007: A tornado destroys the town of Erolville, Kansas.

1 June 2007: Helen moves to Sydney.

2 June 2007: President George W. Bush makes a surprise visit to Iraq.

3 June 2007: Ray is arrested for drunk driving, after showing a reading of 0.08.

5 July 2007: Helen finds job working in a call centre.

24 July 2007: Boris Yeltsin dies.

25 August 2007: Ray appears in court, loses his licence for six months.

29 August 2007: Mudslides kill 102 in Bangladesh.

29 August 2007: Ray loses his job.

15 October 2007: Ray calls Helen's mobile phone.

16 October 2007: *Harry Potter and the Deathly Hallows* goes on sale.

16 October 2007: Ray calls Helen's mobile phone.

17 October 2007: Ray calls Helen's mobile phone.

18 October 2007: Michelangelo Antonioni dies.

18 October 2007: Helen changes her phone number.

19 October 2007: Ray calls Helen's phone for the last time.

20 October 2007: Ray calls Cassandra's mobile phone.

1 November 2007: Thailand votes for new constitution.

13 November 2007: Cassandra and Ray move in together.

14 November 2007: Helen begins Masters in Communications.

15 November 2007: US Attorney-General Albert Gonzales resigns.

25 December 2007: Helen leaves her parent's house when Cassandra arrives. Ray spends Christmas alone.

1 January 2008: Three suicide bombers kill 124 people in Baghdad.

19 January 2007: Helen is asked out by Edward Fairfax, teacher at the school she works in. She refuses.

3 February 2008: Cassandra and Ray argue.

5 February 2008: Cassandra and Ray argue. Cassandra leaves.

12 March 2008: Space shuttle Discovery launches for a twelve-day mission to the International Space Station.

16 May 2008: 33,000 people evacuated from Mexico City due to serious flooding.

11 May 2008: Helen enters sole application for divorce, on grounds of irretrievable breakdown.

16 May 2008: Ray burns Helen's clothes.

12 July 2008: Cassandra and Ray reunite.

30 September 2008: Divorce granted by the court.

1 November 2008: Helen asks Edward Fairfax out. He accepts.

10 November 2008: 7.9 magnitude earthquake kills 73 in Japan.

14 November 2008: Helen completes Masters in Communications.

1 December 2008: Helen gets job as subeditor at Harlequin Press

4 December 2008: Leona Helmsley dies.

21 December 2008: Ray and Cassandra argue. The police are called.

27 December 2008: Study released by Colorado University finds that 72% of second marriages end in divorce.

22 December 2008: Edward proposes to Helen. She accepts.

LAST WORDS

Every morning when Auld woke up, his left arm was dead. As he turned on the light and rubbed the feeling back into his fingers, he thought of his wife, Susan. When she was alive, she had prodded and poked him to prevent him from sleeping on his arm. Auld yawned and picked up a large-print book from the bedside table, but after glancing at a few pages he threw it aside, realising with annoyance that he had read it before. Every week he went to the library and spent an hour deliberating over which novel to borrow and each time, after he went home and read thirty or forty pages, he became aware he had read the book years ago. Shaking his head, he took the pen and notebook that lay on the bed beside him and wrote up his forgetfulness. Auld had been a doctor and was monitoring himself for signs of a final decline. He had borrowed the idea from a character in a novel, the name of which, somewhat ironically, he could no longer recall.

For an instant Auld didn't recognise his handwriting, which had aged with him, the letters leaning over and wandering off the lines like confused old men. Then, although it was still dark, he stood up and drew back the curtains. Opposite his house was a decaying corner shop where years ago he used to get his morning paper. A placard beneath one of the broken windows proclaimed a ten-year-old headline that was as unchanging as a tombstone. The walls of the shop were a palimpsest of graffiti. A dying building's last words were always curses, Auld thought.

He went into the bathroom and looked in the mirror. Auld had a thin face, with deep straight lines of wrinkles, like a map that has been folded and unfolded too often. After washing himself with a frayed flannel, he was careful not to step in the water that had spilled onto the tiled floor. He hadn't realised that growing old would require cunning, how the ordinary town he had lived in all his life would suddenly become seeded with deathtraps. Stairs, potholes, cracks, rain, tufts of grass. Any of these might trip him, leading to a wound, infection and death.

When he returned to the bedroom he saw it was becoming light outside. An old man went by the window, walking his dog. Now that Auld was old, the world seemed full of old men. He put on his dressing-gown and went out onto the driveway to fetch the newspaper. It was a chilly morning and the sky was the colour of a cataract. He sat in the kitchen with a cup of coffee and completed the crossword puzzle, timing himself. Dutifully he noted he was a full two minutes behind his average time from the previous year. He looked through the newspaper, pausing at articles which described fatal accidents and murders. One item caught his eye. In Gloucester, a young tiler had died after falling from a roof. Auld wrote in his notebook, 'Mark Higgins (d. 18 July 2007): "I think I'm OK."'

Auld had always wanted to write a book and his theme had come to him years ago, at one of the many deathbeds he had attended. He had started to record the last words of not just the famous, but also the unknown and the ordinary. Susan had found his project too depressing and had forbidden him to work on it. But her last words ('Did you turn the iron off?') were at the bottom of page twenty-one of his first yellow notebook, and he had filled four more since she died. He had once planned to type his notes and send them off to a publisher, but he knew he would never do that now. Most last words, he had discovered, were banal. There were few 'Rosebuds'.

He read the world news as he ate his breakfast, then put the newspaper to one side, untempted by the illicit thrill of the obituaries. If someone he knew had died, he would learn of it later when he went to pay his respects to his old friend Billy Chatters (whose last words had been, 'Remember – your best friend is the last dollar in your pocket. When that's gone, you have no friends').

Auld's bones ached. He was seventy-two. Sometimes he thought of the patriarchs in the Old Testament who had lived for nine hundred years. God had been merciful and shortened man's lifespan since then.

He put on his suit and a black tie and spent a long time polishing his shoes, stopping only to go to the toilet (the third time in an hour). He put his notebook and pen in his jacket pocket, along with his hearing aid. Then he took his walking stick and locked the front door. He walked very slowly down the street, realising he had become one of those old men he had often noticed when he was young, who moved so slowly you wondered how they ever arrived anywhere. The bus stop was only a hundred yards down the road but it took him fifteen minutes to reach it, and even then he arrived out of breath. Soon a bus came and he got on. It was almost full and the talk of the other passengers irritated him. If he was able, he preferred to sit behind old Chinese couples, or ancient Greek men, happy that he couldn't understand them. Auld was grateful for Babel falling. The world would be unbearable if you could understand everyone in it.

As the bus shuddered through town, Auld stared out the window. He had lately begun to study ornithology, another task to keep his mind from dying before his body. He could name almost every bird that he saw from the bus: kookaburra and flame robin and even a musk lorikeet. It struck him then that though he must have seen a dead bird at some time in his life, he could not remember the specific occasion. It was as if they didn't die. He knew this thought was nonsense, but it pleased him nonetheless. He stayed on the bus for half an hour, stepping off near the steelworks.

Auld walked up to Billy Chatters' house and knocked on the door. It had no nameplate or number. Billy had joked that this was to make it harder for death to find him. Billy's daughter, a fussy, middle-aged woman, let him in. A few elderly mourners sat on furniture that seemed even older than them, and a fat priest was leading the prayers. Billy had become a Catholic before he died and left all his money to the church. One of the old women showed Auld to the room where his friend rested in an open coffin. Auld paused at the door, remembering the first dead body he had ever seen, his grandfather, sixty-eight years ago. He supposed a first death was as unforgettable as a first love. Billy's corpse was dressed in a new suit and lay comfortably in the white-cushioned coffin. Contemplating him, Auld was sure that he wanted a closed casket for himself. He had told his daughter many times. He had never worn make-up in life and didn't want to start in death.

He said a decade of the rosary, rushing the last three Hail Marys when he realised it was nearly visiting time at the home. Then he leaned over the coffin and placed a dollar coin in Billy's jacket pocket so that wherever he was going, he would have at least one friend. Auld wanted to be on his way, but was detained by the other mourners. They were discussing their doctors as if they were their enemies and they wanted his medical opinion on their various illnesses and treatments. Finally he got outside. In the garden the priest was smoking a cigarette. He shook Auld's hand, saying, 'I'll see you at the funeral tomorrow, God spares us.'

Auld nodded, and said, 'In the end, Father, God spares none of us.'

*

Auld got out of the taxi in front of a large, high-walled building painted a bright blue. A sign beside the gate said 'Sunrise Homes'. Then, in steadily decreasing font, like an eye test, 'Secure Accommodation for the Elderly and Infirm'. Entry required a key for the wrought-iron gate and an electronic code. Auld felt proud he could remember the number without having to refer to his notebook. Ensuring the gate had shut behind him, he walked through a well-maintained courtyard. A pair of old women were shuffling along the path that ran all the way round the home. 'Is this the way to London?' one asked him, and he nodded. By the time they went round the other side of the building, Auld knew, they would have forgotten this one. He went towards a glass door but before reaching it he had to stop and lean against the wall. He had been feeling a painful tightness in his chest on and off for some weeks and now it had returned, worse than ever.

The aching reminded Auld of when he was quite young, perhaps nine years old, and had gone to visit a museum with his parents. One of the exhibits had explained the human circulatory system. There was a model of a heart and a hidden loudspeaker making beating noises, and beside it a rubber bulb which, when squeezed, would move some coloured liquid through a tube. The plaque directed visitors to grip the bulb in synchronisation with the heartbeat. Auld was able to do so for only a minute before his hand began to cramp too much to continue. He was reminded of that now when he felt the pain. He was aware of his heart's weariness.

At last he collected himself. He opened the door after assuring the old women again that they were nearing London. The complex was a converted children's home and the bright yellow wallpaper with murals of cartoon characters had been left unchanged. Auld went past the television lounge, where most of the residents spent their days, watching soaps and dozing. But there was only one old man there now. He glanced mournfully at the clock and announced in a loud voice, '2.45 p.m.', like a doctor calling time of death. At the end of the corridor was a large desk with childproofed drawers. A middle-aged nurse sat behind it.

'Hello, Agnes,' Auld said.

The nurse took her glasses off and smiled at him.

'Hello, Doctor,' she said.

Agnes Connelly always called him doctor, though he had retired years ago. They chatted for a while, and he allowed her to describe her sciatica without showing his irritation. Although Agnes was getting on, Auld would always remember her as a young forty, when she came to his house the month after Frank, her husband, had died of a heart attack. She was the last woman Auld had been intimate with. He remembered the precise date, 10 October 1994, as if it were an important historical event.

Auld heard the man in the TV room exclaim '2.59 p.m.' and he suddenly recalled his promise to babysit for his daughter later that afternoon. He interrupted Agnes's arthritis and began to question her about the residents. With a sigh she bent over, took a piece of paper from the desk and gave it to him.

'Gordon Woods died the other day, and Rose Clarke the day before. I wrote their last words down for you.'

'Thank you,' Auld said, folding the paper and putting it in his pocket. 'And how is Mary today?'

'The same. She's in the playroom,' Agnes said. 'She's waiting at the bus stop to go shopping.'

Auld shuffled to a large room at the rear of the building, full of bright toy cookers and fridges, plastic fruit and colouring books. A very old woman stood by a simple sign that said 'Bus Stop'. She had a shopping bag in her trembling hands and a set of rosary beads tethered to a small Christ on a cross. Auld sometimes wondered what Jesus would have been like as an old man. But of course, he had chosen to die at thirty-three, not seventy-three.

He sat behind a small table and arranged the pretend food in front of him, wooden cake slices and empty containers marked 'Sugar', 'Eggs' and so on. The old woman watched him anxiously until, with an effort, he looked up with a busy air and said cheerily, 'Hello, Madam. How can I help you this morning?'

Mary smiled and said, 'Some eggs please, and butter. Oh, and a toy for my little brother. He wants to be a doctor, you know.'

'Of course, Madam,' Auld said. 'Here you are.'

*

Auld's daughter Helen lived in a large rundown house by a storm drain which always had a trickle of water running through it. The noise, which could be heard in every room, somehow sounded unclean, like the plash of urine in a toilet. Helen invited him to visit constantly. Sometimes he pretended to forget her invitations and sometimes he genuinely did forget.

His daughter met him in the hall. She had a deep voice and a mannish figure and was always dressed in pink – blouse, skirt, shoes – as if to convince the world, and herself, that she was female. Auld felt sorry for her. He knew she would be a frightful old woman. Helen's husband was an unobtrusive man who was often away on business. Auld preferred to visit when he wasn't there, as he spoke to Auld with false enthusiasm, the way a self-conscious man might make conversation with a child.

After she kissed him on the cheek, Auld picked up a framed black and white photograph from the hall table, showing a striking young woman and a beaming man dressed in bathing suits.

'I haven't seen this photo before,' he said. 'Who's that with your mother?'

'That's you, Dad!' Helen said, laughing, thinking he was making a joke.

'Oh. Wasn't I good looking back then?' He smiled, but the slip had upset him. He would have to make a note of it later.

They went into the living room and his granddaughter, Sarah, waddled over to meet him. She was a beautiful, blonde child, charming and utterly selfish. Babbling, she gripped his walking stick. He leaned over her and said, 'It's Papa! Can you say Papa?'

'She still hasn't said a real word yet,' Helen said.

'Not to worry, there's plenty of time for that,' Auld replied, tickling the little girl.

'Thanks for minding her, Dad. I'll be back in three quarters of an hour, before she goes to bed. Are you going to come over to dinner on Friday?'

'At my age, I don't like to make any promises,' Auld sighed.

He could never resist talking of his age with his daughter. She seemed as incapable of imagining him dead as he was, and he found this reassuring.

'Nonsense, Dad,' Helen said briskly. 'You've got years and years ahead of you. You have to help Sarah with her studies when she goes to university, you know.'

After his daughter left, Auld watched Sarah play with some dolls. He tried to read the newspaper but was distracted by the tightening in his chest. Feeling quite ill, he went to the window for some air. He was sweating. Far away, in the dusk, he could see wrinkles of surf sweep over the beach. He turned around when he heard Sarah cry out. Red faced, she bawled and slobbered, holding the thumb she had caught in a drawer. Auld picked her up with some difficulty and started to hum a ragged lullaby. She quieted in his arms and he sat down. Very soon the pain in his chest would become unbearable, his heart attack progressing as methodically as if described in one of his medical textbooks.

'I think it's time for a sleep now,' he said.

THE FOOTNOTE

Thomas Hardie was born in Sydney, on 16 June 1940.[1] His parents weren't great readers and had never heard of the writer of *Jude the Obscure*. When Hardie discovered Hardy, at the age of seven, he insisted from then on being called by his middle name, Edward, so there would be no confusion when his first book was published.

Hardie always spoke of his infancy with regret, because he hadn't been able to read and his parents rarely read to him.[2] Once, he said of his father, 'He was like a book for young children: very thick, but containing only a few simple words.' His parents must have suffered in comparison to the mother and father in *The Swiss Family Robinson*. Often, Hardie wished his mother dead, leaving his father free to marry an evil stepmother.

---

1   This date is the anniversary of Bloomsday. My father spoke of this so often that as a child, I believed Bloomsday was the eighth day of the week

2   When my mother was pregnant, on the other hand, my father would read aloud to her for at least an hour each night. Before I was born I had heard most of Kafka and all of *The Story of O*.

He was disappointed to be given so little material he could use for a Bildungsroman.

At eighteen, Hardie won a scholarship to study English literature at university. He had already read the list of prescribed texts for the next three years, and so he spent his time becoming a poet. He wrote sonnets, odes, elegies, quatrains, clerihews, villanelles, acrostics. Searching for inspiration, he tried to take to drink, like Dylan Thomas, but he always vomited after his second whisky. He even bought some marijuana (he insisted on calling it opium) from a flatmate, hoping to emulate Coleridge. But it only made him anxious. Cultivating eccentricity, he stole his clothes from fictional characters – a greasy raincoat from Father Brown, a silk dressing-gown from Bertie Wooster, a shabby necktie from Bill Sykes.[3]

He walked everywhere. Hardie hated cars and buses and could barely tolerate bicycles. On street corners he would seem always to be looking around for a Hansom cab. He liked to read as he walked, measuring his speed in chapters an hour. At night he would write his essays, usually finishing them an hour before they were due.

After gaining an honours degree, Hardie briefly considered becoming a teacher to support his writing, until, by chance, he read *Sons and Lovers*. Appalled by Lawrence's description of teaching, he decided to try something else. His father, who worked for the council, arranged an interview at a local library. For the occasion, Hardie memorised a fifteen-minute speech tracing the history of book borrowing from the destruction of Alexandria

---

3   Often I would see my father glancing at himself in the mirror, posing for author photographs that would never be taken. He was a vain man, yet his fascination with himself was somehow innocent, like a baby looking at its own reflection.

to the infinite library of Borges. As it turned out, he was only required to arrange a dozen books in alphabetical order, and he got the job. That night, he began to write his first play.

Hardie had been working at the library for three years when he met Julia. He was busy stacking books when she appeared in Fiction. She was pretty, but her features were too symmetrical to be beautiful. Her face appeared exactly the same looking from left to right as right to left, like a palindrome.

He asked her what she was looking for, and she told him, 'Something by Thomas Hardy. Do you know him?'

Hardie usually left a long silence before answering a question, like the blank pages before the start of a novel, but this time he answered immediately.

'Yes. As a matter of fact I do,' he smiled. 'That's me.'

He asked her out at once, and that night they went to a dance-hall.[4] They talked about the novels they had read and Julia was impressed when Hardie told her he was a playwright. She was in Sydney to visit relatives and was returning to Queensland the next week. They saw each other every day, before Julia tearfully left for Cairns.

Abandoning yet another play, Hardie composed a twelve-page letter to Julia. She wrote back immediately, and they continued to correspond almost every day for four years. He plagiarised every love poem he could find in the library, from Horace to Robert Browning. After fifteen hundred letters, Shakespeare proposed for Hardie and Emily Dickinson accepted for Julia. They were married the following year and moved into a large house three streets from the library, soon filling it with almost

---

4   My mother and father danced before me only once, on their eleventh wedding anniversary. They were like two strangers trying to pass each other in a narrow corridor.

as many books as the library itself. Finding that they had less in common when they talked than in their letters, they would leave each other little love messages, hiding them in a purse, under a teacup, or in a book.

Both Julia and Hardie were virgins when they married. Hardie, who was by now head librarian, used his position to borrow a number of books from the university's restricted section. With great earnestness, in their first years of marriage the couple attempted every position listed in Burton's translations of the *Kama Sutra* and *The Perfumed Garden*, though Hardie could never persuade his wife to contemplate *Venus in Furs*.

Hardie began to write short stories. The very first he submitted was accepted by a small literary journal based in Perth. He always said that this was the happiest day of his life.[5] Unfortunately, the magazine went bankrupt before publication of his story and they failed to return his only copy. Still, the acceptance encouraged him, and in the next few years he wrote over two hundred short stories, literary at first, but then Westerns, Fantasy, Horror, Romance, War. None were published. Julia saved all the rejection letters, reusing the paper for shopping lists or to jot down telephone messages.[6]

At home, Hardie spoke less and less. Sometimes, when he finished a story, he would become more cheerful, but inevitably, a day or two later, there would be a rejection waiting for him on the mantelpiece. Julia, meanwhile, talked constantly, but her

---

5   I was born two weeks earlier.

6   My mother sometimes gave me these letters to draw on. In the evenings when my father came home from work he would see his failures scrawled over in red and yellow crayon, rocket ships blasting off from the 'Dear Mr Hardie, We are sorry ...' My father always took my pictures and, after a glance, put them in his briefcase.

words were only another kind of silence. They divorced[7] after twelve years of marriage. There were no arguments. They simply stopped leaving messages for each other.

Julia moved to a small flat only a mile away from the old house. She and Hardie resumed writing to each other and once more they fell in love with each other's letters. But they had learned their lesson, and despite living so close together, they never saw each other again. Now that he was single, Hardie decided he had the time to become a novelist. Alone in the house he was able to write at all hours, and in the months after the separation he completed one hundred and twenty pages of his novel, the first of a planned sextet. Then Julia died.[8]

For many years, Hardie continued to work on his interrupted novel, spending his days at the library,[9] thinking over the plot, and his evenings writing. He would sit at the kitchen table, amongst the dirty dishes and cutlery, sipping at scalding cups of coffee. Steam would mist over his glasses at every mouthful and he would have to wait a few seconds before he could go on writing. On the rare occasions when he left the house, Hardie always carried a book with him to read as he walked. Once, waiting for a bus, he realised he had forgotten his novel. He took a ten-dollar note from his wallet and, squinting, began to read *The Man from Snowy River*, printed there in

---

7   I was four years old.

8   My grandparents on both sides were dead, so my father had little choice but to take me back. From this time, he called me 'Porlock', after the visitor who disturbed Coleridge when he was composing *Kubla Khan*.

9   My father would take me to his work every day and leave me in his office with a pile of picture books. I was always very quiet. In fact, after my father's house, the library seemed noisy.

minuscule type. As time passed,[10] he spoke even more slowly, his head tilting to the left, as if he were reading out the titles on a bookshelf. He took to wearing a suede coat that he never washed, and when anyone commented on it, he would laugh and say it was his dust jacket.

At the age of fifty, Hardie had a minor stroke. He quickly made a full recovery, save for his left eyelid, which noticeably drooped, like the corner of a page turned down to keep the place. In a few weeks he returned to the library on a part-time basis. At home, he began to spend all of his free time in the basement, sorting immense piles of paper into thick cardboard boxes, which he would then carefully label: 'Juvenilia 1946–50', 'Letters, March to October 1968', 'Collected Plays', 'School Report Cards'[11] and so on. He bought a computer, had it connected to the internet, and for a month was often online, researching and compiling notes. One day, intending to look up some information about a specific year, he typed in '69' and watched the screen fill with images of naked men and women.[12] Although he could read the most explicit descriptions of sex without blushing, the pictures repelled him and he never used the computer[13] again. 'Orwell was wrong,' he said in disgust. 'If

---

10   After I learned to read, my father began to take more interest in me. When I had mastered *The Cat in the Hat,* he presented me with a copy of *Tristram Shandy.* For the next year, I had to read aloud to him from Sterne for one hour in the evenings.

11   I started secondary school shortly after my father's stroke. Upon returning from hospital he began to scrutinise my history marks and to buy me history books, all covering the Australian post-war period.

12   As a teenager, under my bed, instead of pornography, I kept James Bond books.

13   It was on this computer that I would write my essays when, at my father's insistence, I studied history at university. He insisted on proofreading my work, often rewriting it. I always received higher marks for the essays I wrote on my

you want an image of the future, imagine a man ejaculating on a woman's face, forever.'

Three years before he died, Hardie retired. He had become an old man swiftly, the way a character in a novel can age twenty years between paragraphs.[14] His dust jacket was stained with coffee and even when he wore new clothes, they seemed sec-

---

own. To prevent his interference I set him bogus questions which he would spend months researching. I always made sure to give him a distinction.

14   After the graduation ceremony, my father took me down into the basement. I hadn't been there for years. The bundles of papers were all gone. He had finally finished his cataloguing. There were perhaps fifty neatly labelled boxes stacked against the walls and he had made space for two old armchairs, his typewriter and a tape recorder with a microphone.

'What's this?' I asked.

'It's for the interviews, of course,' he said. 'You're going to write my biography. Sit down, Porlock.'

He had realised that if he would never write a book, then at least he could become one. He wanted me to embalm him with words.

'I thought we'd begin with my childhood,' he said, easing himself into one of the armchairs. 'That's the first four boxes beside you.'

Sickened, I thought of the months it would take, the years, and the futility of it. But I knew that if I said no, that one word would be crushed by the millions crammed in the boxes surrounding me. So I just shook my head.

'What?' my father said. 'Are you saying you won't do it?'

I shook my head once more.

'You selfish little bastard,' he said. But even in his anger I thought I could see a trace of delight that, after all these years, one of the thousands of characters he had created had done something that surprised him.

He turned away from me and tapped out three words on the typewriter.

'I want you to leave now, Porlock. You're just a footnote in my autobiography. And that's all you'll ever be. Now get out!' he shouted, and I left.

ond hand. In the daytime he was restless, always going for long walks with one novel or another, though he had lost the knack of it and had slowed down to a mere twenty pages an hour.[15]

Hardie was killed by *Huckleberry Finn*. He was reading Twain's novel as he crossed a busy street, and a car struck him. Despite the force of the impact, which threw him ten metres, he still clutched the book in his hands, his index finger marking the place where he died, on a raft, floating down the night-time Mississippi.[16] He was seventy. The funeral service was held at a small, ugly Anglican church near the library where he had worked for so long. He had chosen the readings himself, but instead of the King James, the minister read from the Good News Bible, which would have infuriated him.[17] There were few mourners. Most of the people Hardie considered friends, such as Michel de Montaigne and Henry James, had died hundreds of years before.[18] During the drive to the cemetery it started to rain with a heavy-handed symbolism Hardie would have detested. The service was brief and soon the plain coffin was covered with dirt.[19]

---

15   I would follow him sometimes, as he trekked through Zenda or holidayed in Costaguana, standing beside him when he stopped at street corners, out of breath. Sometimes our elbows would, just barely, touch. But he never looked up from the page.

16   I learned of his death from the newspaper. It announced itself in his own voice, for the voice that I hear when I read words, any words, is my father's.

17   He had had his revenge years before, when he would order me into bookshops to remove copies of the Bible from 'Religion' and place them in 'Fantasy'.

18   I carried a paperback *Oliver Twist* in my pocket so that Dickens, at least, could attend.

19   After the funeral, I returned to my father's house for the first time in years. Down in the basement, all of the boxes lay open and university essays, letters,

... and closing the front door behind me, I read on the tarnished nameplate, 'T.E. Hardie.'[20]

---

notes, littered the floor. I searched for my childhood drawings, but I couldn't find them. The typewriter held one page which said 'I was born' and nothing else, as if, after seventy years, this was all my father could say for certain about his life. I added a full stop, and walked up the stairs. For the last time I left his house...

20 My father.

THE EXAMINATION

MINEDUC S3 English Examination Answer Sheet

Date: 21th June 2000

Name: Hakizimana, Stephen

School: Kabahini Secondary School, Umutara Province

ID #: 463290573

This examination consists of three sections, A and B and C.
Answer ALL questions, barring other instructions.
Time allotted: 2 hours.

A) Grammar and Vocabulary

Write a sentence in conditional I, in the negative form.

If I do not pass this exam, I will not become a S4 student

Circle the correct answer. There is only one.

(Karangwa went at home.)
Karangwa went to home.
Karangwa went in home.

Write a sentence using verb + prep.
The others students **make** fun **of** me because I am so big

'If Hope had arisen earlier, she would have been in time for school.'
Rewrite beginning, 'Had ...'
Had Hope had arisen earlier, she would have gone to school.

Correct the mistakes in the following sentence. 'At our country, elec-
tions are held each two years. We are very proud on our free elections.'
In our country, erections are held every two years. We are very
proud of our free erections.

Write a sentence using the superlative form of old.
I am the oldest/eldest boy in the school.

B) Reading Comprehension

Read the passage on sheet 3, 'Scrabbling for Words', and answer the
questions on the bottom of sheet 3 below.

ANSWERS:

1. It is a game made by Butts, Alfred, American, but game
   also played in our Rwanda.
2. Champion of world of 1979 (my birthdate) was France, Jean
   Destre.
3. True
4. True
5. 1260 points
6. 'to scratch frantically'
7. i) Yes, I have ever played this game Scrabble.
   ii) With my father. He buys me this game when I 1st
      learned to read English, and he could not, but he moves

tiles around and asks me to spell out letters.

iii) A Scrabble dictionary. I have this with me in the
refugee camps where I am lost for five years, but only
the eight letter words part is there, so I study and know
many eight letter words. There are so many of these
words like LOVINGLY, MERCIFUL, and
OPTIMISM, and my father's name, INNOCENT.
There is also GENOCIDE.

8. Butts, Alfred was an architect which was his dream job.
My dream job is (please PTO there is no space here.
Answer is after Composition)

C) Composition
Choose from one of the following topics and write 500 words on it.

A wedding you once attended.

Our country, Rwanda, faces a difficult future in the
increasingly complex socio-political climate of the 21st
Century. What actions should our leaders take to remedy
this?

'When a strong wind blows, the palm trees bow to pay
homage.' Discuss.

Yes, I attended a wedding and on the one hand it is a very good
wedding and on the other hand it was a very bad wedding, this
wedding of my brother and his wife. To set the ball rolling,
my name is Stephen and I am Rwanda. I am very black with
white eyes. I am somehow fat and broad and short, but my
three brothers were tall and thin, and my sisters were none.
My father was humour and a peasant farmer. He owned three
'milk machines' (cows). Every morning we all walk up at half
six o'clock. We plant and farm sweat potatoes and Irish potatoes and some bananas. My father and my mother work hard

to send us to school. Our father gives us a push to the end of the ramshackle road every morning to say that goodbye.

Our village is called Video because you can see films there. It is in the land of a thousand hills, which is also the land of a thousand problems. More to that, my older brother Prosper was getting married to a beautiful girl. She has the eyes of a young cow (Rwandan compliment.) It was my first time to go to a wedding. On wedding day we all get up and prey to God. I brush my tooth and wash my hairs. I collect firewood and water and my father buys Fanta and goats to eat. Eh, my friend! So many people were moving up and down in the village that day for the wedding of my brother. In the morning we all pray football, and break fast. Then suddenly the radio says that 'You must to kill the *inyenzi*'. Which is Rwandaise for cockroach, which is what Tutsi are sometimes called and we are Tutsi. My father is eating beans and making a humour noise with his bottom, and my mother shouts at him and we all laugh. At twelve noon we all go to the church. The priest joins my brother and his wife together. Then there is a feast under the trees. We all take Fanta and converse with one and other. But on the radio, the president's plane exploded, and the radio said that now is the time to stamp on cockroaches. My father stood up and said to all of us that 'Give me your identity cards' and he took them all and put kerosene on them. My mother said 'Don't!' and my father said, 'We must, isn't it?' and he burnt the cards.

Furthermore, the gorillas came. I remember these gorillas all the days of my life. There are/were a baker's dozen of gorillas (13). They all had *pangas* (machete) and some had long guns. The leader of them wore sunglasses and had no eyes. The second little ugly fat gorilla was hard to tell if he was a man or a woman. He was like a worm (i.e. androgynous). It is a cockroach wedding, the fat one said. Where are your ID cards (identity cards)? They shouted. (The cards have Hutu and Tutsi on them, and they want to kill only the Tutsi.) We don't have cards, my father said. It is OK said the gorilla, we will have an examination. We can see who is cockroach by looking, and he pointed with his panga at my mother and my three brothers and our cousins and our neighbour who is Tutsi too and the fat one said, Come and we go, and took them into the church. And the others he said were Hutu and let them go.

Henceforth there was only my father and me and the gorillas and the big gorilla said, What is this one? You are a Tutsi, isn't it? Here, he points at me. And my father said, no he is a filthy Hutu like you, look at him, he does not look like me. I don't believe in you, the big gorilla said, and so my father expectorated on my face (This is a biology word, meaning spit with saliva.) He is not Tutsi my father said, he is not. And the gorilla said, Go, and I went into the Nature and I hid.

At the end of the day, all things considered, when I came back after some time I looked in the church and it was full of cadavers. All my family and friends were there. I wept many tears from my eyes.

In conclusion and final to that, it was the worse wedding. And that is 700 words.

*

8, continued. My dream job is to be biologist teacher. Biology is the study of life and nature. There is no genocide in nature, only human nature. In biology there are five kingdoms (which is not to include Kingdom of Heaven, where is my family). I want to teach that people are not cockroaches, and there is no Hutu and Tutsi only Homo Sapiens. And for that I must to pass this exam. Then I will be happy, everyday.

Now, full stop.

STUDENTS: DO NOT WRITE BELOW THIS LINE.
IT IS FOR MARKERS ONLY

A: 5/10 B: 4/15 C: 9/10 Final Mark: 18/35 = 51%
PASS

UNDERSTAND, UNDERSTOOD, UNDERSTOOD

'I don't understand, I'm sorry,' Greene said, as he looked at the picture of the corpse. 'Was this your husband?'

Elena, his landlady, smiled at him, her hand half-covering her mouth and the gold communist dentistry. She was large, forty-five, and had long dark hair which she tied back with an elastic band. She always wore dark clothes and had a pleasant, sad face. Greene felt he could understand it. She carried herself as if she knew she wasn't a woman men looked at, and he knew this because he wasn't a man women looked at.

Elena handed him another photograph of the blue-suited body in an open casket, then one of the man, resurrected and smiling in the poky room where they now sat.

'*Vyras?*' Greene asked.

Elena leaned forward.

'*Kaip?*' she said.

Greene pointed to the word 'husband' in his phrasebook and Elena nodded. After passing the book back and forth between them for a few minutes, Greene concluded that Elena's husband had also been a teacher. Handing him a note, Elena said something in Lithuanian. Greene recognised the handwriting. It was one of his Year 5 students. The note said *Please do not use so much hot water when you are washing one's self.*

Greene nodded. He had lost count of the notes she had given him since he had taken a room with her five months before. They had begun nonsensically with *Mr! Polite request to not leave platters in the bassoon*, but had gradually improved in grammar and spelling until he could now almost always understand them.

Before him on a small coffee table was breakfast, a plate of cold hotdogs covered in chopped onions and tomato sauce. As Elena brought him more tea, he looked out the window at the quiet road and the square with the empty plinths where Lenin and Stalin had once stood. The next photograph was of Elena and her husband outside a snowy church on their wedding day, smiling with closed mouths. Greene finished his breakfast and said slowly, 'I have lessons. I must go.' Elena saw him to the door, which came open after she closed it and had to be closed again. Then he walked out into the cold.

His walk to work went: the street, the lake, the market, the school. But just to be sure, Greene carried maps of the town he had asked his students to draw for him the week he arrived. He had become so used to their distorted scale that he sometimes left himself ten minutes too long for the walk to school, situated as it was at the edge of the lined notepaper. His students had told him that in Soviet times maps had been designed with deliberate errors, streets that led nowhere, to confuse foreign spies.

After three inches' walk, according to the map, he came upon the frozen lake. Four burly, crew-cut young men were smoking on a bench nearby. Greene had seen them before, shouting at the town's one black man, an African basketball player. Greene skirted the lake, went through the deserted market and arrived at the school, a large, low building he suspected was built with asbestos. He went to the staffroom and shook hands with the four teachers there, only one of whom, Ruta, spoke English. She was a very fat woman with a thin face, as if her body were starving it. Greene disliked talking to her, for she paused long over even the simplest questions, as if struggling to render an obscure pun into the unfamiliar language.

'How are you?' he asked her.

'I am normal,' she said after a lengthy silence. Greene explained to her once again that the correct response was 'Fine'. Ruta could speak several languages and insisted on teaching him phrases in Esperanto during the breaks between lessons. Greene had been to dinner at her house once and had seen pictures of most of her family in their coffins.

The bell rang and he went to class. The whisper *Angliskai* followed him down the corridors, as the students he didn't teach peered at him. 'English,' they called him, and he had never bothered to correct them. He didn't even know the word for 'Australian' in Lithuanian. The floor and walls of the school were painted a dull olive. Once, Greene had visited the former interrogation cells of the KGB in Vilnius, which had been painted precisely the same colour.

His students were waiting, twenty-three of them. Standing when he entered the classroom, they chorused 'Good morning, teacher.' They were fourteen or fifteen years old and some of the boys had hairs on their upper lips, while the girls were pretty and shy. Greene had a good memory and knew their names, their dream jobs, favourite colours, family trees and what they had done during the summer holidays. Yet he could only recognise them under certain circumstances. If Eglé wasn't sitting with fat Asta, if for instance he saw her walking in the street alone and she greeted him, he wouldn't know her.

He started the lesson on the weather. He knew they found his name amusing and he told them he was thinking of changing it to Blue, it was so cold. Some of the class laughed, while the others waited for the joke to be translated.

As he went on, all but one of the students eagerly listened to him. Robertas was a lanky, lazy boy. Greene had never heard him speak English, though every lesson the boy wore clothes with English words on them, some of them obscene. One day Greene had told Robertas to change his T-shirt because of what it said, but the boy asked him (in Lithuanian) to first explain to the class what it meant. Greene had gone wearily back to the past simple. Now, when he asked him what the weather was like today, the boy smiled, shrugged and looked away. His friend whispered the question in Lithuanian and Robertas said something which made the class laugh.

Greene stared at him for a moment, then asked another student. 'It is chilly,' she said. 'Very chilly.'

The lesson went badly after that. They asked him questions about diphthongs and gerunds and he didn't know the answers. For the rest of the morning he taught 'At the Doctor's' and 'Ordering Food'. He gave them 'malaria' and 'dysentery' and 'spaghetti bolognaise'.

He had three more lessons that day, then he walked back to his flat in the dark, shivering. Elena had also returned from the school. Greene opened one of her physics books but he couldn't understand the equations. She saw him reading and leaned over him to explain something. He let her talk for a full five minutes before he said once more, 'I don't understand.' After dinner she handed him another note, written by the same student as before. It said, *Would you like go with me to visit the agreeable attractive coastline tomorrow?* He was about to refuse, when Elena said, 'Please?'

Greene had never heard her speak English before.

'Yes,' he said.

She woke him with a knock on his bedroom door early in the morning. They walked in the frost and dark to the bus station, past old women sweeping aside the new snow with birch brooms. It took three hours to reach the Baltic Sea and Greene dozed for most of the time. The landscape was as flat as the rest of the country – what his students called mountains were no more than hills. They arrived in Palanga in time for lunch and ate thick black bread in the garden of Thomas Mann's summer house. Then they went out together on the dunes of the spit, and it began to snow on the sand. Elena started to talk and he didn't stop her, although sometimes he would look in his guidebook as they walked along, to read about the shifting dunes, how a house might be swallowed in one night. The villagers had learned to build their front door in two halves, in order that the top half could always be opened if the sand crept up unnoticed in the dark.

At some point Elena took his hand. She wanted to take a photograph of him with her ancient camera but he wouldn't allow it. He didn't want to end up in the same album as her husband. It was already getting dark and they returned to the bus station. They travelled back to the village in silence, and when they reached the flat she handed him another note. It was in neat writing he didn't recognise at first. Then he realised it was her own. The note said, *Please to sleep with me.*

Elena took off her thick gloves and touched his cheek. Her hands were very warm. In bed she wouldn't stop talking and he lay awake for a long time afterwards, listening to the sound of her voice.

They spent the Sunday morning together. After lunch Elena tried to teach him some of her language. She found the phrase 'I'm sorry, I don't speak Lithuanian' in his phrasebook and drilled him until he knew it by heart, then he teased her by replying in only those words whenever she spoke to him.

He didn't have lessons until late on Monday afternoon, so he lay on the couch for most of that day with his phrasebook, practising nonsense to amuse Elena. Then he dressed in more clothes than he believed he had ever owned in Australia and went outside into the falling snow to walk to school. He taught two lessons, one for Year 11, Robertas's class. The boy still couldn't understand him, or at least pretended not to, and wouldn't answer even 'Hello' or 'How are you?' But today Greene didn't care. He stayed for an hour in the staffroom to finish some marking, closing the door twice behind him as he left. He realised that this was how he would think of Lithuania, a country where every door had to be closed twice.

Then the walk back to the flat: the school, the market, the lake, the street. It was dark as he passed the lake and the four young men, smoking on the bench. They called to him and he smiled and shouted over his shoulder the phrase Elena had taught him, 'I'm sorry, I don't speak Lithuanian.' When he was tripped by one of them he thought he had stumbled into one of the phantom streets of the communist maps. At first they punched him around the head, and then they started to kick his stomach. Greene screamed 'Help! Help!' until a snowball was stuffed into his mouth and he retched. The whole thing lasted only a moment, then the youngest one leaned over and spat in his face. '*Rusiskai*,' he said. They took his wallet and left him.

Greene lay in the snow for a long time, his face and chest and right hand pleasantly warm. Then he was on the stairs to the flat, though he couldn't remember walking there. In the heat the frozen beard of blood around his mouth and chin began to melt and he bled. Elena found him on the floor in the hallway and ran for the retired doctor next door, who called for the ambulance. The doctor insisted on speaking to Greene in French. Greene repeated the last two words of anything he said and this seemed to satisfy him. Soon the ambulance came and took him to the hospital. They examined his bruised ribs, shone lights into his swollen eyes and splinted his broken index finger. The retired doctor drove them home in his old Lada and Elena helped Greene into bed. He slept all the night and next day and would say nothing when she spoke to him. Sometimes he ate what she brought him, at other times he turned to the window.

On Wednesday morning Ruta came to visit with a young policeman. She translated his description of the men, inaccurately, Greene was certain. Before they left Greene asked her what Rusiskai meant. He waited for her to form a reply.

'It means Russian,' she said at last. 'Perhaps these men, these hoodlums, thought that you were Russian.'

A little later Elena came and sat at the foot of his bed. She had brought him some beetroot soup, which he left untouched by the window. Very slowly and carefully, she said to him in English, 'I love you.'

Greene said, 'I don't understand. I'm sorry. I'm very sorry. I don't understand.'

He looked away from her as Robertas always looked away from him in lessons, and after a while she left the room. The door came open again and Greene got out of bed and shut it. The next morning he dressed slowly and carefully, taking care not to look at himself in the mirror. Then he took his textbook and limped to school, passing the place where he had been beaten. The hollow of his body in the snow had been trampled over by children who had rolled a pinkish snowman there. Greene went to the staffroom to fetch the roll and met Ruta. He assured her he was ready to teach again, that he could still write on a blackboard. As he was leaving, she asked, 'But really, how are you?'

'I'm normal,' Greene smiled.

In the classroom the children went quiet when they saw him. He wished them a good morning and asked them to open their books at page 143. Robertas was looking out the window.

'Open your book please, Robertas,' Greene said. 'Page one, four, three.'

The boy didn't obey and mumbled something, smirking. His friend said, 'He says he does not understand.'

'Robertas, open your book,' Greene repeated slowly.

Robertas winked at him, and was beginning to speak in Lithuanian when Greene slapped him hard across the face with the textbook. The tears started in the boy's eyes and the blood in his nose. Immediately, he opened the book at page 143.

'Now he understands,' Greene said. 'Now we all understand.'

JULY THE FIRSTS

It is July the first.

And Ernest Hemingway is cleaning his favourite shotgun, the one with the silver-edged barrel, which he will place in his mouth the following day, and Nostradamus has died and Sir Thomas More is on trial for his life and I (1970–present) am lying awake in Newcastle. On this day Vespasian was given the purple by the Egyptian legions and Napoleon captured Alexandria. The first television advertisement, for a watch, was broadcast in New York City, costing the Bulova company nine dollars. It's 12.50 a.m. In 1971, in a Brisbane hospital, my wife Sarah has just been born. Four years ago at this time I lay in bed awake, listening to her stir beside me. She wanted to make love, but I said I was too tired. By then I already knew the history of her body, the provenance of every scar and blemish.

This year (2004), I have taken to sleeping in old piles of the *Newcastle Herald*, which I bought from a pensioner in Charlestown. The past week I made my bed with the 1989 earthquake and reports of genocide in the Balkans, but tonight I can't sleep and so I continue work on the introduction to *The History of Newcastle*.

My handwriting has filled ninety-two notebooks stacked in piles along the walls, while bookshelves hold the hundreds of history books and journals that are referenced in the sixty pages of footnotes. And I haven't even arrived at the First World War. I once wrote a history of Africa that took less research than this account of a small Australian city. Yet I'll always believe I was born to be an historian, exiting from my mother backward, in order that I might better understand where I came from. I turn a new page in the introduction (p. 104) and write, 'Abraham Lincoln once said, "We cannot escape history."'

The Beatles start singing 'Paperback Writer' on the radio, number one today in 1966. There are more songs and I stop writing and listen to them: 'My Foolish Heart', 'Why Don't You Love Me'. When 'Guess Things Happen That Way' begins I run barefoot to turn the music off, trailing a Lambton murder from 14 December 1983 on my heel. My feet are dirty. The floor is filthy with my dead skin and hair. Historians shouldn't sit in ivory towers after all.

It's 5 a.m. on July the first and in 1993 I had just proposed to Sarah. We lay in bed together in an Edinburgh hotel. I had bought the engagement ring the previous afternoon at an antique shop. I wanted it to have history. Sarah said it was the best birthday present she ever had. She told me of the men she had loved before and asked me about the women I had been with. 'I don't want our pasts ever to come between us,' she said. I had a bad cold that night, I remember. My medical history: measles (1975); appendicitis (1984); a fractured left arm (1992); malaria (1993, 1994); and of course, clinical depression (2001 to present).

It's a cool morning. Leaving the house, I cross the street and walk past the undertakers, where an Australian flag is displayed against black curtains. My house is near the harbour. The roof was once destroyed by a Japanese submarine that fired thirty-four rounds at the city on 8 June 1942. Three drunken young men shout at me and I hurry past them, thinking of the first day of the Battle of the Somme.

I walk to the foreshore and look out at the ocean. In the pale light I can see five identical coal ships spaced equidistant along the horizon, like a time-lapse photograph. Long ago today the French frigate *Medusa* sank, the survivors escaping in a raft, which became stuck in the sea of the famous painting. There's a strong smell of seaweed. It's Estée Lauder's birthday. In 1998 at this time I was asleep in a Melbourne hotel room, but not with my wife.

I walk back and forth along the sand for a while then return to the road, charging up San Juan Hill with Roosevelt to take my street without casualties. It's eight o'clock in the morning on July the first and I haven't slept. I return to bed and watch old black and white films for hours, looking for Olivia de Haviland to wish her happy birthday. Then it's midday and the postman rings the doorbell and I wait until he rings again, in honour of James M. Cain, also born this day.

The postman is a sweating Barbarossa of a man. Ink has come off on his large hands as if he has been making words with them. He has a package for me. It contains more history books, including one that I wrote about the Mau-Mau rebellion. Years ago I lent them to Sarah's sister, but I need them now for my history of Newcastle. Sometimes I think I'll need every history book, from the time of Thucydides to those yet unwritten.

When I open one of the books a photograph falls out. It has been so long since I have seen one that isn't stapled, captioned and dated. A man and a woman are standing outside a dark stone cathedral. The picture was taken on July the first 1989 in Glasgow, when I met Sarah for the first time. I could hear her in the basilica before I saw her. She was leading a group of Polish students. Her Australian accent I recognised at once, but there were certain other words she pronounced differently, some rising unexpectedly, some falling. I imagined numbers over these words, leading to footnotes which explained that she had once lived in China, India, England. I watched her, fascinated. When she talked about the past she threw her hand back over her shoulder, when she spoke of the present she pointed in front of her, and the future was a sweeping gesture of both her hands. (She used these movements in class to give visual clues for tenses, and they had become habit.) After sending her students away to look at a tapestry she sat down to read her book on a bench outside. I saw she had only a few pages left.

'What are you reading?' I asked her, and she looked up at me.

'A biography. Jane Austen,' she said.

'Oh. Is it a happy ending?'

'Well, she dies,' she said, and we laughed.

I remember how her hands moved when we arranged to meet the next evening. Later, I watched her students sing 'Happy Birthday' to her. The next year, we were alone when we celebrated.

In 2004, now, I return to the one hundred and fourth page of my introduction. Outside, above the houses, there's a picture of the sun in the sky that is already some minutes old. I wonder how it compares to the sun the Americans made in the Bikini Atoll, the fourth time the atom was split, years and years ago. After some time writing, I fall asleep. When I wake, it's 5 p.m.

In 2001, the conference on African history I was attending in Sydney had just ended. It was Sarah's birthday and after having a drink I was going to call her, to tell her that I would be home soon. There was a black woman sitting at the hotel bar. I knew she was Burundian from the speech she had given about French colonialism. Her name was Clio Mbabazi. She was very attractive and invited me to join her. 'It is July the first,' she said, 'and Burundi is celebrating its independence.' She looked at my wedding ring and my whisky. 'And so, it seems, are you.' I called Sarah at nine o'clock to wish her happy birthday and to tell her that I wouldn't be home that night, as we had planned. There was too much work to do.

At this moment I am hungry and I eat using 23 November 1997 as both tablecloth and napkin. The bread is four days old, the cheese is six days old, and I am 12,575 days old. I go to shower off the history of the day. The ink, the sweat, the dirt. It's still July the first, still, and Marlon Brando has died, though he's there on television screaming, 'Stella! Stella!'

I sit on the floor and something cuts into my leg. Sarah's diary. I have read it several times, appearing in its pages as an historical figure, like a Garibaldi or a Caesar. Herein all my lies and infidelities are recorded. 'Surprisingly, for an historian,' Sarah wrote on July the first 1999, 'my husband feels no shame about fabricating the past.'

Suddenly, it seems, it's 10.02 p.m. Exactly three years ago I was in a hotel. On the radio, Johnny Cash was singing. I kissed Clio Mbabazi and we took off our clothes. Afterward I couldn't sleep and I flicked through the Gideon's Bible. Much later I learned that the Gideon society had been formed on a July the first by some Wisconsin travelling salesmen.

It's 11.41 p.m. and in 2001 Sarah is dying on her thirtieth birthday, alone in our bed in Newcastle. A heart attack. The doctors were surprised. There was no history of heart disease in her family. If only someone had been with her, they said, she might have been saved. In Germany, Chekhov was dying too. They would take his body back to Russia in a crate marked 'fresh oysters'. Like Shakespeare, whom Chekhov greatly admired, Sarah was born and died on the same day.

Abraham Lincoln once said, 'We cannot escape history.' It is July the first.

THE SAVED

Mrs Watt stepped down awkwardly from the bus, her head aching with the sound of the loud hymns on the staticky radio. She wore a blue sarong and a white blouse discoloured by sun and sweat, and her long grey hair was tied up under a straw hat so children wouldn't be tempted to pull it. She was wearing sunglasses, as she always did. Otherwise, the peasants would stare into her eyes and she could never make them look away.

She rested briefly where the road met the lake. In the evenings, after lessons, she had often swum there with Daniel. She was about to go on when she noticed a baptism taking place. A dozen solemn women dressed in white robes stood knee-deep in the calm lake. Their pastor was in water to his waist, with a pious expression that suggested he could have walked upon it had he wished. The first woman waded in and after a few words, the pastor immersed her. Two men were on hand to carry the woman to land, stricken as she was with the Holy Spirit. Mrs Watt was struck once more by how Australian her God was, how middle class. The water had turned the thin fabric of the woman's robe transparent and her large breasts and dark nipples were obvious.

Mrs Watt noted that the next two women to be baptised, while similarly moved by the spirit, still had presence of mind enough to cover their breasts as they were dragged from the water.

Mrs Watt continued up the steep hill that led to the school. Lines of young women walked past her with baskets of potatoes or cabbages on their heads, and in the shade the men held hands with each other like lovers. They all watched her. Sometimes she felt that when she finally left Rwanda she would linger on as an afterimage whenever someone blinked. Halfway up the hill she passed through the school gates. As usual, the old man guarding them scowled at her. Today he was wearing torn jeans and an acid-green T-shirt that proclaimed, 'The bigger the BOY, the bigger the TOY, the bigger the JOY'. He stood beside the sign with the school motto, 'Struggle to become literate'. Mrs Watt looked up, breathless now, to see when she would reach the first classroom. She had started to limp, suspecting she had a jigger in her foot. In this country the worms wouldn't wait until you were dead.

A schoolgirl looked out of one of the glassless windows to watch her slow march up the hill.

'Ah, teacher! Where have you been all these days?' the girl called to her. 'You are lost!'

'Hello, Faith,' Mrs Watt gasped, resting against the wall. 'What are you doing in there all alone?'

'I am not alone, teacher. God is with me,' Faith said.

'Of course. Of course,' Mrs Watt said. 'What are you writing?'

'It is an essay for the Bishop's English class,' said the girl. '"What is Fashion?"'

'Ah, yes,' said Mrs Watt. She leaned through the window to peer at the girl's exercise book.

'"Short skirts lead to sexual relations between boys and girls, hence prostitution,"' Mrs Watt read aloud. '"Bare shoulders lead to sexual immortality, hence prostitution." Mind your spelling, dear.' Mrs Watt spoke kindly, though she didn't like the girl. Faith had murdered her family for five extra marks in a test, lying about a massacre in her village so Mrs Watt would feel sorry for her and let her pass the S3 exam.

'Faith, did you know Mr Daniel was arrested?' she asked abruptly.

The girl nodded.

'Did you tell the truth about him?'

'Yes,' Faith said, looking down at her essay. 'He forced me to play sex with him.'

'*Have*,' Mrs Watt corrected her absently. 'We say have sex, not play sex. You wouldn't tell a lie, would you? It's very serious.'

'I swear to God,' the girl said, raising her right hand. 'I cannot lie. I am saved. Are you saved also, teacher?'

'Saved?' The old woman smiled. 'I don't know, Faith. How do you know if you are saved?'

'The Bishop told me. I am saved. Master Daniel is not saved. He was a pagan, and even then he sometimes praised with the Adventists who worship on Saturdays. They are all damned, the Bishop says.'

'Do you think God is a calendar that he cares so much about which day we worship?' Mrs Watt said sharply. But of course the girl did not understand. 'Goodbye, Faith,' she smiled, 'I must go. I have an appointment with the Bishop.'

Mrs Watt left the girl alone in the classroom with her God and went on limping up the hill. Dehydrated, she stopped to rest for a moment, turning round to look down the steep slope. She had found the best way to think of Rwanda was to imagine it as a postcard, cheerful farmers and graceful women balancing baskets on their heads, and not to concern oneself with what was outside the edges of the picture. In this case she had cropped the genocidaires who were working on the road that led to the teachers' houses. One of them wore a loop of grubby white cardboard around his neck and was leading the other prisoners in prayer. On the edge of the postcard, Mrs Watt could glimpse her own small mudbrick house and the garden she had stopped tending when her digging brought up bones.

She hobbled past the other classrooms, long brick buildings all facing towards the administration block. It was Thursday afternoon and the children had lessons. Mrs Watt saw her students in Biology. They sat three to a bench in their simple uniforms. Carved on their desks were mathematical formulae, English irregular verbs and the dates of battles in the American Civil War. Mrs Watt had gone to great trouble to learn the names of all her hundreds of students, although their biblical nature had come to weary her. There was another Faith sitting there, she saw, and nearby two Hopes and a Charity, who all detested each other. The boys were mainly Joshuas, Aarons and Calebs. Daniel should have taught this lesson. Instead it was one of the Bishop's friends. He was drawing on the blackboard something Mrs Watt at first took to be a diagram of a nervous system, but which was actually Adam and Eve's family tree.

A boy slipped out of the classroom and walked with her up the hill, listening to his portable radio. 'Hello, how are you, I am fine,' he said. Mrs Watt knew she ought to send him to the Bishop for skipping class, but instead she tried to keep up with him so she could listen to the BBC on his shortwave. There was a competition to discover the African of the decade and a listener from Ghana had suggested, without irony, AIDS. Then there was the proverb of the day, 'In a town where the cats are barbers, the mice must go around with long hair.' At the pips marking the hour, the boy turned the radio off and went into one of the latrines. Mrs Watt took a pot-holed path to the left and was soon at the administration block. It was a new brick building and a cracked wooden sign above the door said, 'KABAHINI SECONDARY SCHOOL'. Each of the words were a different colour, one of the o's in 'school' floating untethered from the rest of the sentence, a pink afterthought. At one corner of the sign had been added, 'With God, all things are possible'. Mrs Watt suspected the Bishop wanted this to become the new school motto.

She stumbled on an uneven step at the doorway, the bricks crumbling where she steadied herself. The staffroom was a narrow trapezium with a small window placed strangely at waist level. A generator chugged noisily out back and the light from the one feeble bulb left the spidery corners unbrightened. There was a long desk and four wooden benches of the kind the students used, a noticeboard and two small green doors, which led to the offices of the Bursar and the Bishop. Mrs Watt knocked on the Bishop's door, but there was no reply. She slumped on a bench and waited, thinking of Daniel. She had first met him here, two years ago. He had been reading a history of the world when Mrs Watt came in with the Bishop. He had stood when the Bishop introduced him, a foot shorter than her at least, and shook her hand energetically, as if he were straining water from a pump. Daniel had a delicate, handsome face and a thin moustache that he liked to comb with his fingers. He had grinned when she asked him what class he was in. 'A student? Oh, Mrs Watt! I teach Biology, not to mention Physics, Chemistry and Ethics. I am twenty-six years old. The life expectancy here is forty. I am middle-aged!' His voice seemed older than he was. She recalled how it would carry from his class to the staffroom, talking of zygotes, stem cells and especially loudly of reproduction and contraception. Daniel knew how much this annoyed the Bishop.

There was a new, messily gestetnered notice pinned to the board. Mrs Watt got up to read it.

> All schoolgirls! If your hair is bigger than middle-finger length, it will be cut by me, personally. Long hair equals party girls, hence sexual frenzy and Hell. Your headmaster/Bishop.

Through the window she saw the Bishop himself, scissors in hand, pursuing three shrieking girls past the pit latrines. He was a slight, very clean man, who always wore a beige suit and white shoes which never seemed to get muddy, even in the rainy season. He was sweating as he caught one of the girls by the arm and cut rough rectangles of hair from her head, so that she would have to have the rest shaved. The girl started to cry. Wiping his face with a pristine handkerchief, the Bishop saw Mrs Watt through the dirty window of the staffroom. 'Through a glass, darkly, Mrs Watt!' he cried. 'Please, wait in my office.'

Mrs Watt sat on a small stool in the Bishop's office, which was only a little larger than a cupboard. Multicoloured timetables were nailed to the plywood walls and several pictures of a very white Jesus gazed down at her. The Bishop's desk was bare save for a heavy copy of the Bible in Kinyarwanda and two lighter editions in French and English. Mrs Watt had once seen the Bishop give a sermon in five different languages. She was embarrassed that her God only spoke English. Beside the window was a framed piece of embroidery, presented to the Bishop by the Archbishop's wife. It was the first lines of William Blake's 'The Little Black Boy'.

> *My mother bore me in the southern wild,*
> *And I am black, but oh my soul is white!*

The Bishop kept her waiting almost another hour, and Mrs Watt passed the time by reading Exodus. 'Forgive, forgive,' he said at last as he came in. He had a habit of leaving long pauses between each word as if he expected God to interrupt him at any time. 'When I said to meet at three o'clock, I should have said African time. We Africans are not as punctual as you whites. If I had made this appointment with a Rwandan, they would still not be here!'

Excusing himself past her, he sat down. 'But Mrs Watt, my friend, you are lost these days! You are very lost. Where have you been?'

'I went to Kigali, to make enquiries about Daniel.'

She had gone to the Ministry of Education to discover if they knew where Daniel was being held. In the end she had been seen by an official working in a small office with the word 'Educaton' on the door, as if it were part of a satire. The man could tell her nothing

'Oh, Mrs Watt, I said I would look into that for you. Now, isn't it?' the Bishop said.

'Yes. I'm sorry, but I felt so useless. And I still do. No one could tell me where Daniel was, or when he would be tried. I must say, Your Grace, I have some doubts about the truth of these accusations against him.'

'Slowly by slowly, Mrs Watt, as we say here. Master Daniel is one of my teachers, and I will save him from this trouble if he is innocent. Though we have had our differences, God knows.' He smiled. 'Slowly by slowly. African time, isn't it? Surely God must be African; it can be such a long while before he answers our prayers. Let us both implore God's intercession for Master Daniel.' He rested his hands on the French and English Bibles. Mrs Watt knew he punished students by beating them with the Bibles. The students feared the Word of God in their own language the most. The Bishop bowed his head and muttered a short prayer. Then he stacked the Bibles together at the side of his desk.

'Have you ever noticed the Kinyarwanda Bible is much bigger than the English? Perhaps God has more to say to the Rwandese. We are terrible liars. Now, Mrs Watt, has anyone been telling you lies about me?'

She shook her head.

'Good, good. Do not listen to rumours. We have a proverb here. "Beans are like people. They talk behind your back!" Now, leave this Daniel business to me. It will be resolved soon, I assure you. Please, you should rest after your journey. I will send the Bursar to your house with some *matoke* in a little while, so you don't have to cook. It is a very tiresome trip from Kigali. Hills and potholes and so on and so forth. But before you go there is a letter come for you.'

The Bishop produced a grubby envelope from a file beneath his desk. It was postmarked three weeks ago and had a Rwandan stamp where Mrs Watt had expected an Australian one. She thanked the Bishop and left, walking carefully back down the hill to her little house by the football field, where some cows were grazing. Her living room contained a wooden bookcase for her grammar books, a plastic chair and a small table. In the bedroom there was only the single bed with a knotted mosquito net hanging above it. The crucifix on the whitewashed wall had come unstuck again in the heat and lay on the dusty concrete floor.

Mrs Watt sat down with a sigh. She could hear the woman next door lullabying her children. She listened for a while, almost falling asleep herself. Then she remembered the letter. Inside the envelope was a child's exercise book, such as her own students used. On the front cover was printed the inevitable 'With God, all things are possible,' but 'God' was crossed out and 'money' was written underneath. Mrs Watt recognised the writing at once.

She turned to the first page and read,

Dear Catherine, I am not guilty. This I swear. I have been in prison for weeks now. They say that I am play-ing sex with schoolgirls, but those girls are like plants to me, that is asexual. Now I am in prison, like Oscar Wilde the writer whose book you lent to me. It is very terrible here. There are hundreds of us in a room no big-ger than my old classroom. There is a smell, flies, disease and death, hunger, thirst. My neighbour, a genocidaire, has a rotten foot. His middle toe fell off this morning. He carries it in a matchbox. Can you imagine?

It has been months now, and maybe you have forgot-ten me, because you are not here. I have written letters before, to you, to the Ugandan embassy, but nothing. Yet I will not surrender.

There was a knock at the door, startling her. She hadn't locked it and she expected it to be the food the Bishop had promised her, but instead three of her students came in, three Marys. Two of them had patches of hair missing. Mrs Watt knew them well. In an angry moment, she had christened them the 'Bloody Marys'.

'What is it?' Mrs Watt snapped. 'I'm very busy.' She could see they had their exam papers with them, and she remembered that she had caught them cheating.

All three of the girls were saved and they implored her, hold-ing out their papers with the red lines across them, 'We are sorry. Forgive! Forgive!'

'I forgive you,' Mrs Watt said quickly. 'I forgive you. But you still get nothing. Now goodbye.' And she closed the door on them.

The girls went away, giggling, and Mrs Watt returned to the letter.

I am a biology teacher by training as you know. Five years have I been teaching in this country, this Rwanda. I am from Uganda, a civilised country, and I am not saved. They have put me in a frame because I was not a Christian, but I am half a Christian now. I believe in Hell at least, for I see it when I look up from this paper.

It is a conspiracy, Catherine, such as destroyed great Africans I told you about, like Nkrumah and Lumumba. I discovered that the Bishop was coercing female students into selling their bodies for no school fees. I composed a letter to MINEDUC (i.e. the Ministry of Education) but little did I not know that the Bishop suspected this and told the policeman (who is his cousin) and had me arrested. As you once told me Shakespeare said of Richard the III, the Bishop can smile, and murder whilst in the process of smiling. Last night I dreamed that this Bishop was baptising me in the lake. But he held my head under and under the water and I drowned.

They want me to recant what I have said and then they will release me and I can return to Uganda. I will not. The truth will make me prisoner, but it is the truth. I am a biologist. I know madness awaits animals in captivity. I beg you Catherine, write to your ambassador, and the Minister of MINEDUC, he may listen to you. But please be careful. Remember, there are no Christs in this place, only Judases.

Your friend,
Daniel.

A long time passed before Mrs Watt got up and fetched her old tape-recorder. Months ago, she had made a recording of Daniel reciting Kipling's 'If' for a listening exercise in class. She played the tape through several times, looking at the photograph of him that she kept in her purse. She had told herself it was to show officials in her search but she knew this wasn't true. After a little time, she dozed. When she awoke, it was growing dark. She had always thought there was a kind of defeat in the sunsets here. The light gave in so quickly. She listened to Daniel's voice once more. He was a very good reader. When Mrs Watt had decided to come to Africa, a part of her had wished for martyrdom, but there was only discomfort: sunburn, mosquitoes, dirt. She had found her martyr now.

Outside, some students walked past on their way to the cathedral. It was almost time for the evening service. Mrs Watt went out, taking Daniel's voice with her. But the batteries faded before she was halfway up the hill, and she abandoned the recorder under a tree. The English teacher in her had already composed a speech in which she would stand and denounce the Bishop for what he had done. The night was black and Mrs Watt went slowly until she came to the path to the cathedral. It was the largest building in the village, square and ugly, and lit up with dozens of bulbs.

There were perhaps three hundred people inside. The only whites were her and the Christ on the cross. A peasant woman gave Mrs Watt her seat and she sat down, forgetting to thank her. The walls of the cathedral were pitted with bullet holes and she thought of the hundreds who had come here during the genocide to be saved, and were not. The Bishop appeared on the altar, grinning. The congregation stood and sang and clapped. Mrs Watt stayed seated as the applause died down and the Bishop spoke for some time in Kinyarwanda. He was extraordinarily pleased with himself; it seemed he was already in Heaven. Every so often he would wipe his forehead with a handkerchief, exclaim, 'Eh! My friend, I tell you!' in English, and then continue. Mrs Watt recognised the words for 'teacher' and 'thief' and 'liar' repeated several times. And then she cried out, as Daniel walked onto the altar.

He had lost weight, his head was shaved and his moustache was gone. He looked like a child. While he had been given dirty brown trousers, he still wore the pink shirt of the prison. He walked slowly to the Bishop's side and shook his hand, holding his own wrist, a sign of deference.

'We have a new member to our congregation tonight!' the Bishop said loudly, in English. His smile was as wide as the wound in Christ's side above the altar. 'He was a trusted teacher in this school, yet in secret he was a pervert and a pagan. He preyed upon young girls and told wicked lies about myself until he was put into prison.' The crowd tutted loudly. 'But now he is saved, and he has come to ask your forgiveness. Then we will fare him well back to his homeland of Uganda. Mr Daniel!' Daniel stepped forward and knelt. Mrs Watt trembled.

Daniel gulped visibly and then shouted, almost screamed, 'I am a liar and a fornicator! Bless the Bishop! Forgive me! Forgive! Forgive!' When he saw Mrs Watt, he hung his head and whispered, 'Forgive.'

The Bishop raised his arms, but before he could speak, the tin roof of the church began to creak and crackle. Within seconds the din had grown until it seemed pieces of sky were raining down. The Bishop bellowed silently above the kneeling sinner, the rain forcing him into comical mime. Mrs Watt got up and hurried outside. Instantly, she was soaked. She ran down the hill, her clumsy progress captured in flashes of lightning. Before long, she fell into a puddle in front of a small hut and lay panting face down in the mud. She felt a hand on her arm. 'Can't you leave me alone, for Christ's sake?' she wept. When she looked up she saw it was the old man who minded the gates. He knelt beside her. She realised then that his perpetual scowl was a scar. Noticing her stare at his mouth, he tried to smile, saying one of the few Kinyarwanda words Mrs Watt knew, '*Panga.*' Machete. Muttering, he helped her to her feet. Mrs Watt allowed him to lead her into the bare hut, waiting with him as the water fell from the heavens. When the rain finally stopped she thanked the old man and offered him a hundred francs. He shook his head and called out to a passing student. The boy came over and the old man spoke to him in Kinyarwanda. The boy laughed and said, 'He says you are the first white he has ever spoken to in his life, up to now. He says that he sees you wearing a cross and going to the cathedral. He just is curious. He is asking, are you saved?'

'Tell him no,' Mrs Watt said as she stepped into the darkness, 'I am not saved. Tell him I am lost.'

TYYPOGRAPHYY

When **Da** came down
                    stairs this morning, **he** was happyy because
of the greyy skyy. **Da** is Scottish, which is whyy I call him **Da**
and not **Dad**, but **Mum** was alwayys **Mum** and not **Ma**.

'Amyy, what are yyou doin wi yyour mother's tyypewriter?'
he asked me.

'It's not a tyypewriter, it's a word processor,' I said.

'Be careful with it. It's old.'

'It's alreadyy broken. The yy keyy doesn't work properlyy.
When yyou press it once, it tyypes twice. Whyy is that?'

'Because yyour mother was like yyou. She was alwayys askin
whyy. I think she wore it out.'

I don't sayy so, but I think **Da** has some worn-out keyys too,
like t and g. **He** sayys 'no' instead of 'not', and 'havin, bein, doin'
instead of having, being and doing. I love to listen to **Da**. For
weeks after **Mum**'s funeral **he** said almost nothing. When **he**
did speak the words were so frail that I used to imagine a platform underneath them to help them stand up.

'<u>It's been a terrible blow to us, terrible</u>,' **he** would sayy. '<u>For
Amyy most of all</u>.'

202

But now **he** doesn't need a line under his words and some-times **he** even smiles, like todayy, because of the skyy. **Da** loves overcast dayys because theyy remind him of Scotland. **Da** works in an ice-cream factoryy in Carrington and doesn't ever feel cold. **He** wears shorts and a T-shirt with a St Andrew's cross on it all yyear round, and laughs when anyyone sayys the word 'Winter'.

'One dayy this week,' **Da** said as **he** started to make break-fast for us, 'I'll get into yyour mother's studyy and start goin through all those letters. I suppose I'd better write to tell them that... To tell them that she's gone.'

Mum had penfriends from all over the world and **she** would write to them on a word processor, because her handwriting was so bad. **She** taught me how to use the machine before **she** died. I used to write myy diaryy on it, and everyyone I loved would be in **bold** and everyyone I didn't love would be in *italics*.

I learned to tyype twentyy-five words a minute, but **Mum** could tyype as fast as myy heartbeat. **She** let me playy with the word processor and I spent hours experimenting with tyypog-raphyy, a word **she** taught me. I believed for a long time that tyypographyy meant the geographyy of tyyping. I thought of it as exploring the insides of consonants and vowels, fighting off colons and hunting herds of O's with sharp ///'s. But I know now that tyypographyy just means how a page looks. **Mum** used to sayy that all interesting words have boring meanings, and **she** knew a lot of words. **She** would spend hours in her studyy writ-ing to orphans in Africa and political prisoners in Brazil. I don't think **she** had manyy friends in Australia.

Da talks about **Mum** all the time and so do I. But even when we're not talking about her, we talk about her.

'Would (I) yyou (miss) like (her) some (todayy) porridge?' **Da** asked.

'YYes, (me) please (too),' I said, watching **Da** in the kitchen. **He** is alwayys distracted, alwayys reaching for the wrong thing two or three times – ~~cereal~~, ~~bread~~, oats. ~~Salt~~, ~~pepper~~, honeyy. **Da** is a tall man, and **he** has red hair and blue eyyes. I have myy brown eyyes and hair from **Mum**.

We ate the porridge together then **Da** told me to hurryy up or I would be late for school. I've onlyy been back at school for a week and all the teachers are veryy nice to me, even the Maths teacher, *Mr Beaneyy*, with his big round head that looks like it was drawn with a compass.

　　　　　　upstairs and showered and put on myy uniform, then
I ran
Da called me
　　　　　down.

We got into the car and **Da** drove me to school. When we said goodbyye at the gates, **he** kissed me on the cheek and said, 'I love yyou.' For a long time after **Mum** died, **Da** was ⟨Da⟩. It was like **he** had a wall around him and **he** couldn't hear anyything I said. But slowlyy **he** got better and last week the last wall fell down and ⟨Da⟩ was **Da** again.

The first lesson was English with *Mrs Kennedyy. She* is a **woman** of at least 100 kilos and *she* has long dark hair down to her waist, and although *she* is so big, *she* alwayys dances around the room so that the hair swishes behind her like a horse's tail.

'Good morning, everyyone, and todayy I would like to see lots of participation without prevarication,' she said. *She* alwayys uses long words and I think *she* wishes there were more letters in the alphabet so *she* could talk for even longer. *She* wrote 'LOVE POETRYY' on the blackboard and the O was like a zero, so it looked like love had a nothing in the middle of it. We read a poem byy ee cummings, but I didn't answer anyy of the questions and *Mrs Kennedyy* left me alone

because *she* knew about **Mum**. I sat beside **Rachel** and **Beckyy**. Even *Sallyy* has been nice to me since I came back to school. At lunchtime I walked home so I could write about this morning.

*

In the afternoon it was maths with *Mr Beaneyy*, who talks in numbers.

'2748593725,' *he* said to the class, '746583920.'

Beckyy put her hand up.

'946563291?'

'3975316!' *he* said.

Mr Beaneyy likes to stand at the front of the room with his hands on his hips, making two triangles with his arms, and his legs apart making another triangle. I don't think *he* has liked me since the day *he* overheard me sayy that *he* should have been a geographyy teacher because *he* wouldn't need a globe of the world, just his big round head. *Mr Beaneyy* asked *Stephen* and **Alex** a question and, last of all, me.

'164859542. 472524?'

'ooooooooooooooooooooooo,' I said.

'1-0-3-9-7-6-3-4-2-1-7?' *he* said slowlyy.

'o,' I said.

I expected him to get angryy but *he* didnt, *he* just told me to stayy behind after class as *he* wanted to talk to me. After the bell had gone, *Mr Beaneyy* asked me to come to his desk and *he* sat down. His voice sounded different when *he* wasn't teaching, not all numbers. It was quite nice, though I remembered **Da** sayying **he** didn't like *Mr Beaneyy* because *he* was alwayys looking for an angle.

'I just wanted to tell yyou, Amyy, not to worryy about class work this term. I know yyou've been through an awful lot, and two + two is the least of yyour worries.' *He* shook his big head. 'YYour poor mother. Someone so yyoung. It's a tragedyy.'

Up close, I could see that *Mr Beaneyy* had nice eyyes and a lovelyy syympathetic smile so perfect it could have been plotted on a graph. His desk was veryy untidyy, with lots of exercise books and textbooks and folders scattered around, and papers with drawings of rhombuses and hexagons.

'MR BEANEYY, MIGHT I HAVE A WORD FOR A MOMENT?' a voice said. It was **Mr Brown**, the historyy teacher, at the doorwayy, and *Mr Beaneyy* said, 'Excuse me a moment, Amyy. I'll be right back and we'll talk about putting off homework until yyou're readyy.'

I waited for a while, then I picked up a piece of paper to look at *Mr Beaneyy*'s doodles, and underneath there was a folder with the edge of a letter sticking out. I didn't mean to read it, but I couldn't help it because it said in tyyped words, 'Andyyyy dearest,' and I had to see that it was just a spelling mistake, so I picked up the letter and it said, 'Thank yyyyou for the other night. It was wonderful. YYYYou asked whyyyy we couldn't see each other more often, myyyy love, but yyyyou know it's because of him. He doesn't like me being out so often anyyyywayyyy ...'

The yy's. The yy's. **Mum** and *Mr Beaneyy*. **She, she** wrote that to *him*. I felt sick. I stood up and walked out of the classroom and *he* was there and *he* said, 'Amyy?' and I ran ran ran ran ran ran ran ran ran ran ran ran ran ran ran ran ran ran home.

Weuoggggggbhuwoejfjirweij. I put myy head on the keyyboard and I cried. I want to sayy what I feel because it hurts so much, but I can't think of words anyymore. I'll use the thesaurus. Anguish, torment, sorrow, angst, miseryy, gloom. But those words aren't big enough.

Revulsion

Wretchedness

desolation

Myy heart is full of

*

Oh, **Da**. Oh, **Da**. I can't let **Da** know. If **Mum**, if *Mum* wrote letters to *Beaneyy*, then *Beaneyy* must have written letters to *her*. I have to find them. I'm glad now that *Mum*'s heart broke before *she* could break **Da's**.

*

I went to the bedroom and searched in her old wardrobe but there was nothing, and then I threw everyything from her dressing table onto the floor, and the mirror broke, and I pushed the table over to look behind it, throwing clothes everyywhere, and then the studyy where I took all the books from the shelves and opened them, but no words fell out. I pulled the drawers from her desk and looked behind them, and then I noticed a book on the floor that *Mum* was alwayys reading. I remembered her favourite storyy, it was called 'The Purloined Letter'. I read it once and thought it was boring, but I remembered how the letter was hidden in the storyy. There were four shelves of letters from *Mum*'s penfriends, all in alphabetical order, and I just looked for B and there theyy were. I glanced at the letters and I knew *Mr Beaneyy*'s writing, the el that looks more like a one. I tried to read a line or two but I couldn't, and for a minute I was frightened that I couldn't read anyymore. I'm going to take the letters to the fireplace now and burn them one byy one.

*

When **Da** came home from work and saw *Mum's* things broken all over the floor **he** didn't sayy '!^#@%', although I wished **he** would have. For a minute his mouth opened and his lips moved but there was no sound. **He** just said ' ' and that was more terrible than anyy swearing. But finallyy **he** stammered, 'Amyy, what have yyou done?'

'I was looking for more ink for the word processor,' I said. I had written the words on myy hand, so I wouldn't forget what to sayy.

'What?'

'It was running out of ink.'

'Ink?' **Da** said. 'YYou did all this lookin for ink, for that stupid machine and the stupidityy yyou write on it? Look at what yyou've broken. Her mirror. <u>Her jewelleryy box. How could yyou?</u>'

For a moment, **Da's** voice went veryy quiet and I was afraid it would be just like it was after *Mum* died, but then **he** looked awayy and when **he** looked back, **he** was angryy.

'GO TO YYOUR ROOM AND THINK ABOUT WHAT YYOU'VE DONE. NOW.'

So I came here to myy bedroom and shut the door. I could hear **Da** moving around, putting everyything back in its place. Just now, **he** knocked on myy door.

'Goodnight, Amyy,' **he** said. There was silence for a minute and then **he** said, 'I love *yyou*.' In his voice, I could hear the **bold**, but also the *italics*. **Da** still loves me, but **he** hates me too.

I wish I could be a tyypographer, and then I could get lost between c and v. When I think of *Mum*, sitting in front of this thing after we had gone to bed, using the same keyys I am touching now to touch *Mr Beaneyy*, I can't look at it anyymore. It will make **Da** even more angryy, but I am going to pour water on it and destroyy it noewI34HG428 3HR8 Co88o` ooCCCCCCUo` ooCCCCCCU8UJN M S Jehogqhhhhhh hhoq349hrgnaowqiefhhhhhhhhhhhhhhhhhh4oqw"""""""""""""fh hhhhhhhhhhhhhhh-

yyyyyyyyyyyyyyyyyyyyyyyyyyy y y y

THE EUNUCH IN THE HAREM

From *The Sydney Review*, 23 August 1999
The Grass Cadillac
By Frank Harmer
Porlock Press, 96pp, $22
Reviewed by Peter Crawley

Reading *The Grass Cadillac* is a unique experience. It is the first book of poems I have ever read which does not include a single line of poetry. The collection marks the literary debut of Queensland writer Frank Harmer, a name I spent a good half hour trying to rearrange into an anagram of Ern Malley, so sure was I that some trick was being played. But even Ern, I suspect, would not have tried to palm these poems off to an editor, no matter how gullible. To say that the verses in this substantial volume approach mediocrity would be a compliment. Mediocrity does not figure even on the horizon of this book, though ignorance looms large. Harmer has no idea what alliteration or onomatopoeia is, and I suspect he thinks a metaphor is someone who fights bulls.

As an example, let us turn for a moment (though this is being over-generous with our time) to the first poem in the book, 'The Melting Clock'. The title is apparently an allusion to Dali and the poem an elegy to a dead dog, or a love letter to a married woman, I can't decide which. But then, neither could Harmer. The first line is 'Th'e ni'g"ht cas"cades wh"en she's aw"ay / cuck'old, empo'wer ti'll da'y's da'wn.'

This reads like a poem generated by computer, though surely a computer would do a better job. For some reason most of the poems are punctuated in a like manner, with swarms of apostrophes hovering like flies over the dead verse.

Whilst there is nothing that resembles anything so coherent as a 'theme' in *The Grass Cadillac*, the 'poet' himself appears regularly, every two or three pages, like a dog marking its territory. Sometimes he is in the first person, sometimes the second, and sometimes the third, as 'Harmer'. Unfortunately these three people together do not add up to even half a writer. If the reader can progress past the first twelve poems there is some respite to be had in 'To My Coy Wife', at thirteen pages the longest poem in the book and thankfully almost free of apostrophes. The six hundred and eight lines of this epic begin, 'I am comforted by your sock / that I carry into the twilight of luckbeams / held next to my philtrums' and grinds on in the same way, with little rhyme and no reason, reaching its zenith with 'I am filled with hope / that I may dry your tears of semen / so that we may grind as one / labia to labia / in search of the magnificent rainbow of love.'

I will not weary the reader with any more of Harmer's work, though it is tempting to offer a verse or two from the accurately titled 'Shitlines' or a particularly rancid image from 'The Belly of the Dead Baby'. After I had finished reading the collection, I considered not writing a review at all, in order to spare a new poet embarrassment. But Harmer is obviously proud of his work and eager to show it off, in the same way a newly toilet-trained child is proud and eager to show off the contents of its potty.

A great writer once said that criticising a poem was like attacking a butterfly with a bazooka. That may be so, but when the poem is not a butterfly but a cockroach, the critic is justified in the attack. If, as scientists maintain, cockroaches can survive a nuclear bomb, then Mr Harmer's poems will survive the winter of this review. I can only hope they may be driven into the dark, under the floorboards, where they belong.

The most attractive image in *The Grass Cadillac* is the photograph adorning the front cover. The caption on the dust jacket informs me that the bookish-looking man is Frank Harmer himself and the beautiful woman beside him his wife. If that is so, then I can only congratulate Mr Harmer on his luck and advise him that he would be better to concentrate on creating the patter of tiny feet, instead of iambic ones.

*

From *The Sydney Review*, 6 November 2001
The Dog and the Lamp Post
By Frank Harmer
Joseph Grand Publishing, 208pp, $35
Reviewed by Peter Crawley

[The following review was written last month, two weeks prior to the events which occurred at the Newcastle Literary Festival, during a reading of Emma Harmer's poetry. I would like to thank the many readers who sent me get-well cards and the colleagues who came to see me in hospital. I would also like to thank Emma Harmer for her many visits whilst I was convalescing, and for apologising to me on her husband's behalf. I will not comment upon the night in question here, as the police are currently preparing a number of charges against Frank Harmer. My only regret is that the debut of a most promising poet was all but ruined by drunken, thuggish behaviour. Regarding the below review, which, I would like to reiterate, preceded the vicious assault upon me, not one word has been changed or added.]

I am one of those readers who like to write their name and the date on the inside covers of books. I underline striking passages and jot comments in the margins. As a critic, such annotations often form the backbone of a review. After finishing Frank Harmer's collection of a dozen stories, I idly flipped through it to see what I had written and could find only one comment, on page forty-five. 'No tree should have died for this.' This review is an appendix to that note.

Readers may remember Harmer from a collection of poetry published last year, which was reviewed in these pages. Harmer is evidently one of those pathetic species of writers who read their notices. The title of his collection, and the longest story therein, *The Dog and the Lamp Post*, is taken from a comment by Christopher Hampton. 'Asking a working writer what he thinks about critics is like asking a lamp post how it feels about dogs.' It will come as no surprise to all four of the people who endured *The Grass Cadillac* that this image of Hampton's is the only memorable one in the book. Philosophers have long been telling us that an infinite number of monkeys sitting at an infinite number of typewriters for an infinite length of time will eventually reproduce Shakespeare's plays. This I am prepared to concede. However, I cannot accept that an infinite number of Frank Harmers in the same situation would ever come up with an original line.

Harmer, admittedly, is better suited to the bludgeon of prose than the rapier of poetry, even if the only wounds he inflicts are on himself. His stories follow loners and losers, men often burdened with literary ambition but without the talent to pursue it. In 'The Reader of Books', for example, a writer reads his rejected novel aloud to his dying father. In what should be an interesting twist, it turns out that the father has Alzheimer's, and the same two pages of the book are read every night. In the hands of another, this might have been a moving piece. But Harmer could rob even a suicide note of its pathos. His characters obliterate the distinction E.M. Forster made between flat and round. Harmer's characters are square: little boxes half full of dull adjectives.

In 'The Papercut', one of the less tedious stories, a man (Harmer's protagonists are always men) cuts himself with his wife's Dear John letter. Again, an interesting premise is utterly squandered with uninvolving characters and flat prose. Harmer does not understand that the short story is a glancing form. His stories stare. Of 'The Last Night on Earth', 'Rusty's Funeral' and 'What ... What .... What Do You Mean? Exactly?' very little needs to be said. They are a mixture of carved-up Carver and hemmed-in Hemingway.

The longest story, 'The Dog and the Lamp Post', is a thinly disguised diatribe against literary critics and one critic in particular. The main character, Paul Rawley, is a book reviewer for a Sydney newspaper. He is described as having thick, square glasses, a sparse grey beard and a round face which 'resembles a bulldog chewing a wasp'. (Here I would direct the reader's attention to my photograph at the top of the page.) Rawley, an impotent drunk 'who looked like he enjoyed the smell of his own farts', is tormented by the fact that he is merely a critic and not a 'true writer'. It is this jealousy that causes his attempts to ruin the career of a flowering literary genius, Ray Charmer. Eventually (C)Harmer confronts (C)Rawley with a gun and forces the critic to feed on the review, literally eating his own words. To say this disturbing fantasy is the best story in the collection is not to say much. At least Harmer's obvious hatred of critics (and myself in particular) brings the characters lurching to some kind of half-life, and I must admit it was entertaining to see myself caricatured, in the same way it is entertaining, for a moment, to see a child's drawing of oneself. But just as a child's drawing is disposable, so is Harmer's story.

The last three stories in the collection, 'I'm Not Alone', 'The Web of Blood' and 'With the Dead' see the writer take a turn into horror. This is a genre that all too easily descends into the juvenile and the stories here are no exception, though perhaps juvenile is the wrong word to describe such violent, misogynistic tales. The sadistic climax of 'I'm Not Alone' does not invoke uneasiness or chills, as the best ghost stories do, but mere disgust. By the close of 'With the Dead' one begins to worry about Frank Harmer. His writing has begun to resemble that of a mental patient, scrawling his sordid fantasies in excrement on the walls of his padded cell.

It may be some consolation to Harmer that the very few copies of his book that are sold will undoubtedly remain in mint condition. I cannot imagine them ever becoming dog-eared. Once the reader loses his place, there is no desire to get it back. Many of my fellow critics say the novel is dead. If Frank Harmer ever writes one, then it surely will be.

*

From *The Sydney Review*, 29 December 2002
Ariel's Daughter
By Emma Harmer
McGonnigal-Marzials, 16 pp, $15
Reviewed by Peter Crawley
Books of the Year No.4

The announcement of this year's shortlist for the Alexander Poetry Prize caused something of a stir among the Sydney literati when, beside worthy works by David Malouf and Les Murray, there appeared the little known name of Emma Harmer and her slim volume, *Ariel's Daughter*. I was one of the judges of the award and can recall clearly the moment I read her first poem. It struck me like a revelation. Though she eventually lost the prize to Murray, I find that it is Harmer's poems that I enjoy more on rereading and wonder if we judges made the right decision after all.

The title of the collection is an obvious nod to Sylvia Plath's *Ariel*. In a lesser writer, such a gesture would be the merest egotism. But it is no exaggeration to say that Emma Harmer's poems are every bit as luminous, beautifully crafted and extraordinarily realised as Plath's. The sixteen pages which make up *Ariel's Daughter* are at once an encyclopaedia and an atlas. They seem to contain the world and everything in it.

The first stanza of 'A Pen Is Not a Penis' is a strident statement of intent:

> *fuck him who left poor anne hathaway,*
> *fuck him who pushed sylvia plath away!*
> *a pen is not a penis.*
> *when i say this what i mean is,*
> *a dick is not a bic,*
> *a tool is not a tool.*

Not since Greer's *Female Eunuch* has there been such a passionate feminist rallying cry. And yet, Emma's tone soon softens and she proves herself capable of the most sublime thoughts, as in the wonderful haiku 'Reading':

> *midsummer morning*
> *alone at the library*
> *just me and this book*

Its companion work, 'Writing', offers a desolate view of the act of creation, one that will be familiar to any artist.

> *composing cheaply*
> *pen gorges, listless dreary*
> *melody wails, bleak.*

And then there is the magnificently angry sonnet/limerick, 'Editing', in which the poet imagines filling a pen with her menstrual fluid and using it to edit the collected works of Western Literature, removing centuries of sexism and misogyny.

It is a difficult task to quote from *Ariel's Daughter*. I am tempted to continue but this would only result in my transcribing the entire collection. In fact, it is only a respect for copyright that prevents me from doing so. *Ariel's Daughter* is one of those rare books that negate the critic. Essentially, it reviews itself. And with that, I will stop writing.

*

From *The Melbourne Eon*, 2 May 2005
An African Honeymoon
By Peter and Emma Crawley
Xanthippe Press, 192pp, $35
Reviewed by James Devine

An African Honeymoon is the first travel memoir to be written by the *Sydney Review*'s outspoken critic Peter Crawley. Though his wife Emma is credited as co-author, Crawley has let it be known (in a furious open letter) that the half-dozen chapters she actually wrote were excised by the 'Philistine publisher'. Crawley has frequently upbraided Xanthippe Press for 'inaccuracies' in its account of the long-running dispute. This seems unfair, for if anyone has been inaccurate, it is Crawley. The very title of his book is erroneous. Mrs Emma Crawley was still Mrs Emma Harmer when she left for Africa with Peter Crawley in the spring of 2003. The two were certainly not on honeymoon.

The events preceding their hasty departure are described (or rather skated over) in the first three pages of *An African Honeymoon*. Crawley barely mentions the controversy surrounding the 2002 Alexander Poetry Prize. To this day, his fellow judges maintain that Crawley browbeat them into including *Ariel's Daughter* on the shortlist. The controversy deepened when it emerged that one of Harmer's only decent poems, the haiku 'Reading', was plagiarised from the American poet Billy Collins. Harmer's flight from her husband, obscure poet and short-story writer Frank Harmer, is dismissed by Crawley in two sentences. Neither does he record that his sabbatical from the *Sydney Review* was not voluntary, but rather the result of his ecstatic write-up of the execrable *Ariel's Daughter*.

Some of Crawley's more charitable readers assumed this review to be satirical, but on reading *An African Honeymoon* this assumption is swiftly put to rest. One of the surprises of this memoir is that Crawley truly does believe in his wife's genius. In their meandering year-long journey by train (once) car (four times) and plane (twenty-two times), Crawley evidently wishes to play Boswell to his wife, recording her every comment and opinion with reverence. Unfortunately, Emma Crawley is more Dr Pepper than Dr Johnson. She is sweet and bubbly, but too much of her in one sitting makes you feel ill.

When writing of local geography, the people he encounters and the adventures he experiences, Crawley is on solid ground. Freed of the confines of literary criticism, he displays a disarming passion to understand Africa and its inhabitants. His description of wandering through an Egyptian bazaar is wonderfully vivid, as is his alarm at finding himself lost in a rainforest in Uganda. This leads to a superb passage in which a group of villagers demonstrate a warmth and kindness that obviously moves Crawley, even now. His dissecting of the social mores of UN bureaucrats in Liberia is a small masterpiece of sustained venom, while the short chapter on visiting a Rwandan genocide site is both sobering and poignant. Sadly, we do not have Crawley's impressions on South Africa, Madagascar, Sudan or Tanzania, as these chapters were written by his wife and subsequently deemed 'unpublishable' by editors at Xanthippe Press.

I don't doubt that their decision is entirely justified in the light of the Emma Crawley who appears in this book. That she refers to Hutus and Tutsis as 'Tu-tus and Whoopsies' is not charming, as her husband seems to believe, but tactless and crass. Her confusion between the two words 'genesis' and 'genocide' when questioning an old woman in Kigali is horrendously embarrassing, although Crawley strives to present it in a humorous light. Another misplaced attempt at light-heartedness, her referring to the Congo as 'The Fart of Darkness' after a bout of diarrhoea

THE WEIGHT OF A HUMAN HEART

there, falls flat. By the time the couple cross the equator Emma Crawley has developed into a ridiculous figure. With hilarious repetition, everything she encounters in Africa is 'smaller than I thought it would be'. The pyramids, the Sphinx, even Mount Kilimanjaro are described in this fashion. By the end of the book, one is left with the impression that the African continent measures approximately two metres by six.

The couple's return to Australia proves a relief for them, and arguably more so for the reader. *An African Honeymoon* is by no means a terrible book. In parts, it is beautifully written and admirably perceptive. It is also infuriatingly silly and often dull. Still, I find myself in the position of recommending it, for all its faults, as have several other critics in newspapers and journals. Next time, I suspect we will not be so kind. Peter Crawley should take note that in art, as in life, the honeymoon is over.

*

From *The Australian Literary Review*, 29 November 2008
The Eunuch in the Harem: Criticism
By Peter Crawley
Hazlitt-Ruskin Publishers, 656pp, $55
Reviewed by Penny McFarlane

23 October marked the second anniversary of literary critic Peter Crawley's bizarre, violent death at his Sydney home. In a recent press release Hazlitt-Ruskin explained they felt enough time had passed that they could release the first, long-delayed collection of Crawley's reviews and essays. Crawley himself was engaged in the editing of the book when his life was cut short. This edition includes all of his important criticism from the *Sydney Review*, the *Age* and the *Sydney Morning Herald* and the

lectures and speeches he occasionally gave at book festivals. The title of the collection is taken from a remark by Brendan Behan: 'Critics are like eunuchs in a harem; they know how it's done, they've seen it done every day, but they're unable to do it themselves.' Crawley often jokingly referred to himself as a 'eunuch', though many women who encountered him in Sydney's literary scene from the 1970s to the 1990s would be able to give the lie to that. (In the interests of disclosure, I should say that Crawley once made a pass at me at a book reading in Melbourne in 1989. At this time the fatwa against Salman Rushdie had just been pronounced. I can still clearly recall a drunken Crawley, at the end of his speech, announcing the title of Rushdie's next work, *Buddha Is a Fat Bastard*. In the ensuing storm, only an abject public apology saved his job at the *Sydney Review*.)

Since his death, Peter Crawley's name has become irrevocably linked with that of Frank Harmer and the editors of *The Eunuch in the Harem* have acknowledged this by making the twenty pages of Crawley's writings about Harmer the first part of the book. The section opens with the review of *The Grass Cadillac* in 1999 and ends with a dismissive footnote in an essay on Tim Winton in 2006.

To give these writings pride of place is to do Crawley a grave disservice. His criticism of Harmer, whilst amongst his most scabrous, was certainly not his best. For that the reader should turn to the second section, titled 'American Lives'. Here we can find many unique insights into Bellow, Updike and Mailer (who, incidentally, called Crawley a 'Limey asshole' on the one occasion they met, at a book launch in New York). Crawley's analysis of the Rabbit tetralogy has been reprinted several times to great acclaim in the US but is virtually unknown here, and his monograph on Bernard Malamud was highly praised by Harold Bloom. It is a shame to note that Crawley's treatment of Australian authors is spottier. Too often his praise is faint and over-leavened with sarcasm. Still, his half-dozen essays on Patrick White should be required reading for anyone with the slightest interest in Australian literature.

However, it was not Crawley the scholar but Crawley the self-proclaimed eunuch who wrote such guiltily entertaining criticism for the *Sydney Review*. In the longest section of the book, 'A Pig at the Pastry Cart' (another allusion to critics), Crawley selected the fifty of his reviews he felt were most enjoyable to read. Highlights include his opinion on the Booker Prize-winning *Life of Pi* ('It is so terrible I doubt there would even be a place for it in Borges' Infinite Library') and his devastatingly brief summing up of Daphne du Maurier ('middle-class, middle-brow, middling').

Crawley's harsh reviews of Raymond Carver's fiction are surprising, considering the two men were friends. Carver even dedicated one of his final stories, 'Buffalo', to Crawley. But Crawley's dismissal of Carver has a refreshing quality in an era when the American has been hailed as the modern Chekhov. One passage in particular is worth quoting in full:

> [Carver] followed Hemingway's idea of the story as iceberg, that is, only the top one-eighth of life and emotion would be shown, the rest hidden underneath. But in his stories, one can't help thinking that the iceberg is more of an ice cube.

Pleasingly, it is Crawley's evisceration of popular fiction that takes up the most space. His dismissal of Stephen King is brilliantly off-hand. 'To me, his novels are more endearing than scary. King is like a child leaping out from behind the sofa and shouting "Boo!" We don't have the heart to tell him he didn't frighten us.'

As I have said, Crawley's criticism of Frank Harmer is not his best, and it is a sad thing to contemplate that it will probably be his best read. Crawley never envisaged any mention of Harmer in his book. The section 'Thoughts on Frank Harmer' was added after his death. It does not make great reading. The original review of *The Grass Cadillac* was certainly cruel, if undoubtedly accurate. Harmer might even have taken it as an honour to be tarred with the same brush that had spattered Derek Walcott and Seamus Heaney. He was obviously unaware that a review by Crawley, positive or not, would certainly help sell his small book of poetry. Furthermore, if Crawley had been aware of Harmer's history of mental instability, I have no doubt he would never have reviewed *The Grass Cadillac* in the first place. The accounts of their first meeting at a poetry reading are various. Harmer claimed he caught Crawley pawing at his wife and lost his temper. Crawley maintained the assault was entirely unprovoked. Considering the fact that Emma Harmer later left her husband for the critic, many would tend to accept Harmer's account.

Crawley had already filed his review of Harmer's short-story collection *The Dog and the Lamp Post*, but it had not yet gone to press. (Incidentally, he was annoyed that Harmer had inadvertently stolen the title he had wished to use for his book of criticism.) Crawley subsequently claimed he did not change a word of his review, even in light of the broken leg he received. This is true, but it is not entirely to Crawley's credit. As he recuperated, Emma Harmer, on one of her frequent visits, informed him that her husband was being treated for schizophrenia. Knowing this, Crawley let stand the reference comparing Harmer to a lunatic daubing filth on the walls of a madhouse. This was a despicably cruel act from a normally kind-hearted man. Crawley could never forgive Harmer for his very public humiliation and wrote about him again and again in the weeks after the incident. For example, in a review of Henry Boyce's *The Raphael Cipher*, Crawley says, 'Appalling as it is, Boyce's novel has had the good fortune to be published after Frank Harmer's *The Dog and the Lamp Post*, ensuring it will not, at least, be the worst book this year.'

Eventually, Crawley's editor and close friend David Phillips banned him from making any further references to Harmer in the journal. By that time, of course, a scandal had erupted over *Ariel's Daughter*. The original review, at close to 10,000 words, was truncated by Phillips, the two men almost coming to blows when Crawley realised Phillips had cut 96 per cent of the word count. (Phillips later destroyed all copies of the longer version, fearing it would irrevocably damage his friend's reputation.) Even in its shortened form the review is excruciating, reading like a 400-word chat-up line. And yet it must have had the desired effect, for soon after it was published Emma Harmer fled to Africa with Crawley. Her husband, pursuing them to the airport, was arrested for brandishing a knife at the boarding gates.

It is the great irony of Peter Crawley's life that he courted controversy yet married banality. Yet there can be no doubt he was deeply in love with Emma Harmer. Only a man besotted would have so carefully recorded her asinine travel observations in *An African Honeymoon*.

Controversially, Crawley's last, unfinished piece, the essay, 'Whatever Happened to the Great Australian Novel?' has been included in the collection. I believe that here, at least, the editors made the correct decision. The six pages that survive are amongst the best that Crawley ever wrote. Sadly, we will never know the answer to the question he set himself. As Crawley was putting the finishing touches to the essay, a deranged Frank Harmer broke into his house. Harmer found the critic in his study, bludgeoned him into unconsciousness with a glass paperweight, then stuffed the last eight pages of the essay down Crawley's throat, choking him to death.

Peter Crawley once said, pessimistically, 'The good writing about writing will go first, and then the good writing itself.' This collection of good writing about writing has not sold well and the publishers have scrapped plans for a second volume. I'm afraid this will be the last we see of Crawley on the bookshelves, except perhaps in the form of posterity he most detested, that of three or four lines in a book of quotations.

And the good writing itself? Crawley's widow recently changed her name to Emma Crawley-Harmer. Her autobiography, *The Poetess of Sadness* (with its lengthy subtitle, *One Woman's Extraordinary Journey Through Marriage, Infidelity, Madness and Murder*) reputedly sold for a six-figure sum and was released by Picador last week. While the reviews were overwhelmingly negative, the book has debuted at number two on the best-seller list, outsold only by *The Dog and the Lamp Post*, now in its seventh printing.

ACKNOWLEDGMENTS

Several of these stories were written as part of a PhD in Creative Writing at the University of Newcastle, and I would like to gratefully acknowledge the University for its support.

The following stories have been previously published: 'A Room Without Books' and 'A Story in Writing' first appeared in *Meanjin*. 'Africa Was Children Crying' and 'The Eunuch in the Harem' first appeared in *Harvest*, and the latter was reprinted in *The Best Australian Stories 2010* (Black Inc.) and *The Best Australian Stories: A Ten-Year Collection* (Black Inc., 2011). 'July the Firsts' first appeared in *Westerly* and was reprinted in *The Best Australian Stories 2007* (Black Inc.). 'Collected Stories' and 'The Cockroach' first appeared in *Etchings*. 'A Short Story' first appeared in *The Sleepers Almanac No. 4*, 'Anatomy of a Story' first appeared in *The Sleepers Almanac No. 5*, and 'English as a Foreign Language' first appeared as 'The Beginning of the Sentence' in *The Sleepers Almanac No. 6*. 'The Saved', 'The Examination' and 'Understand, Understood, Understood' (under the title 'I'm Normal') first appeared in *Wet Ink*. 'Tyypographyy' won the 2007 Hal Porter Short Story Competition and first appeared in *Award Winning*

Australian Writing 2008 (Melbourne Books). 'The Genocide' first appeared in *Page Seventeen*. 'Last Words' first appeared in *New Australian Stories* (Scribe, 2009), while 'Four Letter Words' first appeared in *New Australian Stories 2* (Scribe, 2010). 'The Chinese Lesson' came third in the 2010 Age Short Story Competition and first appeared in the *Age*. 'A Speeding Bullet' won the 2007 Roland Robinson Literary Award.

Elizabeth Jolley wrote in a short story, 'Writers don't have any friends.' I've been very fortunate to find that this isn't true. The stories in this collection have benefitted enormously from the criticism of a number of good friends and fellow writers. I would like to express my sincere gratitude to Amanda Betts, Patrick Cullen, Erol Engin, Bill Pascoe, Alec Patric, Michael Sala and Laurie Steed for their patience in reading and re-reading these stories, and their invaluable insights, advice and encouragement.

Depending on who you believe, the short story is currently dead, dying or experiencing a rebirth. One thing for certain is that if the short-story form is to thrive rather than simply survive, publishers must give it their support. Black Inc. has been instrumental in promoting short stories in this country over the last decade by publishing the annual *Best Australian Stories* anthologies, and has also advanced the work of some excellent short-story writers through single author collections. I would like to thank Black Inc. for publishing this collection, particularly Denise O'Dea for her tireless work in shaping it and Kate Goldsworthy for getting it over the line. I could not have asked for a more supportive publisher.

I would like to finish with another quotation, this time from Kurt Vonnegut, who said, 'I never knew a writer's wife who wasn't beautiful.' I've been very fortunate to find that this *is* true. This collection is dedicated to my wife Jennifer, for her unending encouragement, her patience, her understanding and her love. All my stories, past and future, are for her.